NEVER LOOK BACK IN TEXAS

An Al Quinn Novel

RUSS HALL

Red Adept
Publishing
Unlocking New Worlds

Chapter One

Sheriff Clayton called Al Quinn a few minutes after six p.m. "I have a little something I could use your help with."

"Hello. Retired. Do you remember?" Al could see Maury and Bonnie out futzing over the grill on the deck that looked over the lake. The smell of hotdogs and hamburgers swept in through the screen door that led to the deck. Tanner was sprawled like a miniature Sphinx at the lower inside edge of the screen, taking in the scents and drooling a little.

Fergie was tossing a salad in the kitchen. Bonnie had wanted potato salad, so it would be "like a picnic." But Fergie was fighting the good fight to stay her lean, lanky, six-foot-two self. She had gotten her hands on some picked-that-morning frisée lettuce at the farmer's market and had added thin slices of purple onion, tomato, and avocado, along with a lemon-juice dressing.

"Are you up to doing a little mentoring?" Clayton asked.

"Not really. Do you recall that the last favor or two you asked nearly got me killed and Fergie along with me?"

"It's nothing like that this time."

"Nope."

"It's just a little thing," Clayton said. "Take one for the team."

"You have detectives in the department who have good experience."

"None with your track record."

"Well, they'll never get it with an old codger like me stomping around while they're trying to learn."

"You're not a codger by any means. You're in your sixties, younger than me."

"When is it?" Al sighed.

"Tonight."

When Al hung up, Fergie said, "You said yes, didn't you?"

He nodded. "He wore me down. I guess we have to cancel our extensive evening plans."

"Do you mean taking me out on the town for dining and dancing? Or the one where we stay home, eat a rustic meal with our roomies, and then curl up with books before going to bed early?"

"The second one."

"Then I suppose you can skip this once. Just don't get yourself shot at, nearly burned up, or anything else this time."

"Okay, though I was looking forward to a good bullet wound or two."

?

"It's just a ride-along," he told himself as he got out of his truck at the sheriff's department. He locked his truck and started toward the waiting unmarked cruiser.

He recognized at once the deputy who had been promoted to detective, Randolph Cannon. But he paused a half-step when he saw that the senior partner who would be training him was Victor Kahlon. Al had helped him far too often in the recent past.

"I thought you upwardly mobile detectives had the cushy day shifts." Al grinned. "Don't you?"

Victor nodded. "Unless some retired duffer of a detective calls us in the middle of the night with some hornets' nest he's stirred up, or if we have to train some new pup, like Randy here."

Randy let out a snort. He'd been a member of the sheriff's department for at least eleven years.

"Just as long as you don't think I'm stepping on your toes," Al said to Victor.

"Hell, I'm halfway to making lieutenant because of you. You can dance the fandango on my shoes, and I'll be okay with it."

"What do you have planned for the night?" Al asked as he settled into the back seat of the cruiser, behind the grill. Neither back-seat door had an inside handle. He hoped he wouldn't end up seated beside an enraged husband after a domestic quarrel, an untamable stray dog, or a young wild boar. He'd had each of those in the back of his department car at one time or another as he put in his thirty years.

Victor chuckled. "We've got to stake out a spread where there's been some rustling."

"What kind of rustling?"

"Emu rustling."

Randy broke loose with a chuckle too.

"Really?" Al asked.

"It could be dangerous all the same," Victor said. "I know you're not usually comfortable unless you're swinging in on a vine with a knife between your teeth."

Randy raised his eyebrows. "Really?"

Al shrugged that off. The sky was just beginning to darken, with the horizon turning pink and orange. He waited a few miles before he asked, "What's the plan here?"

Victor turned in his seat to look back at him. "There's a spread where half a dozen emus were rustled last night. We figured we'd stake it out, see what happens. You've been on many a stakeout in your day."

"Hmm."

"What's wrong with it?"

"First of all, you don't have any stakeout food. I usually have diet sodas and beef jerky at least. Secondly, the odds aren't as good as you think on those things, unless you just like sitting around in a car, staring out at nothing with binoculars."

"What would you suggest?" Victor asked.

"Let me ask you a question, Randy. Who is the likely buyer of rustled emus?"

"I... I don't know."

"Think."

"I don't even know what people do with emus."

"They're just big chickens," Al said, "with a skin that can be tanned into leather."

"I guess, then, that there's some sort of meat-packaging plant the birds have to go to, an emu processor."

"Did you check to see if there are any?"

"No."

"Who else might want emus?"

"I don't know. Someone else who grows emus?"

"Now you're getting warmer. Where are the nearest of those?"

"I don't know."

"You've driven around the county often enough. Where have you even seen any emus?"

Randy shook his head.

Victor finally broke in. "Over on the other side of the county, in between a horse ranch and a goat farm. I've seen emus there."

"I don't go around keeping track of livestock," Randy said.

"Well, you should," Al said, "especially when you're assigned a case where they're at the heart of the investigation."

"Do you care to share with us the usual info dump on this, Al?"

"Okay, if you're sure you want it."

"We aren't. But go ahead anyway," Victor said.

"Texas leads the nation in emus, but the 'new red meat' excitement of emu farming in the nineties went into a downhill slide. The big issue was the cost of the kind of emu processing plant we're talking about. State governments have to approve meat intended for sale in-state. But in order to sell nationally, emu farmers have to process their meat at a facility approved by the U.S. Department of Agriculture. Each processing plant costs nearly a quarter million dollars to build, and there aren't many venture capitalists eager to fund them, because the resulting price of emu ends up being four to five times the cost of simply buying beef.

Even if emu is healthier for people, it hasn't caused quite the splash expected."

"You see why we rarely ask him such questions," Victor said to Randy.

"But where is a plant around here? Should we go there to look around?" A little heat and frustration had worked its way into Randy's voice.

"I doubt the stolen emus have made it there yet. Why don't we check on that other emu rancher Victor knows about?" Al looked out his window as Randy turned the cruiser around. The horizon had turned into a dimming yellow line.

"Did you check with the rustled emu farmer to see if he chipped his birds?"

"What's he talking about?" Randy asked Victor.

"Micro-chipped." Victor reached for his phone. "I'll make the call." When he hung up, he said, "Yep."

"Then why don't we swing by a pet-rescue center I know and borrow their scanner, unless you brought one with you."

"Why do we need it?" Randy asked.

"How else can you tell who the emus belong to?" Al was already looking forward to sending Randy into a bunch of upset emus to check them for microchips.

"A singer-songwriter friend of mine, Marcus Perkins, had a near mishap with an emu once," Al said.

"Do tell." Victor egged him on but kept an eye on Randy.

"Like so many musicians not getting paid what they deserve, he'd taken advantage of a number of the venue's free beers for the band. As a result, he stopped his truck alongside the road on his way home and got out to answer nature's call."

"How's an emu fit into that story?" Randy asked.

"He claims that an emu came up to the three-strand barbed-wire fence, stretched its neck across, and damn near made a eunuch out of him."

"Must have thought he saw a worm or something," Victor said.

"They're prone to grab at shiny objects as well, like a wristwatch or someone's glasses," Al said.

"Okay, you guys. Enough already," Randy said.

Al called ahead, so the stop at the pet rescue center along the way took only long enough for Al to dash inside and grab the pet-chip-reader case from his pal Myra Henningdale, who was still in her office at that late hour. She wore knee-high rubber boots and a rubber apron. Her hair was up in a bun. He didn't have time to ask what she was up to at that hour. She just held out the case containing the reader. He seized it on the run like a running back taking the football from a quarterback.

"Someone lose a dog?" she yelled after him.

"No. Emus."

"If you don't want to tell me, just—" Her voice faded as he shot back out the front door and past a row of kennels, where dogs stirred from their naps to give him a barking chorus.

He ran back out to the waiting cruiser.

Randy stayed within the speed limits and still got them to the other side of the county in under an hour. They passed a horse ranch.

"Is that the emu farm you saw up ahead on the left?"

"Yeah," Victor said.

"Why don't you drive past it, and we'll come back from the other way with our lights out," Al said.

"Really?" Randy glanced into his rear-view mirror. The two-lane road was empty around them.

"Give it a try," Victor said. "Al has a whole bag of tricks. What did you see, Al?"

"I caught just a glimpse of a horse trailer pulled up close to a gate. Some guys were loading something. Since it's an emu farm, I'm guessing it was emus."

"Why is that odd?" Randy asked.

"At this hour?" Victor said. "It doesn't smell right."

"I guess we'll know soon enough how an emu farm smells." Randy turned the cruiser around and headed back the other way. "I've experienced sheep, cattle, and horse ranches. The smell can't be any worse than a pig or turkey farm." He turned off the headlights when they were a quarter of a mile away. At the gate, he turned into the farm. The cruiser's tires crunched on gravel as he eased toward a ranch house, a low, flat barn, and a horse trailer behind a truck with its lights on and motor running.

"If it comes to it, Victor, do you have a judge who could get us a warrant, pronto, should we need one?" Al asked.

"Judge Carter is kind of on call. If I don't wake her up too late and have good probable cause, we should be fine."

"Maybe they'll just cooperate," Randy said.

"Yeah, right." Victor let out a huff of air.

"Let's just wait and keep open minds until we see if anything seems amiss here at all," Al said.

The cruiser rolled up the drive, accompanied by the crunch of gravel beneath the tires. When they were within a dozen yards of the horse trailer, Randy turned on the lights. He stopped the car.

Victor popped out of his side and opened the back door so Al could get out.

A lanky fellow in blue coveralls stepped out of the back of the horse trailer and glared at the cruiser and the men getting out of it. He wore a yellow ball cap with something so faded that it was unreadable on its front. "Hey, no trespassing! It's posted."

"We just have a couple of questions for you," Victor said. He held up his detective's badge.

"Well, you can call them to us on the telephone."

Al eased to the left, looked out into the pasture, and made sure there were emus in the corral by the ramp going up into the trailer's back end.

"Do you mind if I take a quick look at these emus you're loading?" Al said.

"Of course I mind."

"So we can't look at them?"

"I said no." The guy eased off the back end of the ramp and walked over to stand within a foot of Al, who figured him for six foot two or so. Hell, he was used to facing that every day with Fergie. This skinny guy wasn't going to intimidate him just by crowding his space.

Randy had been slower getting out of the car. He stood and ambled over until he was beside Al. "What's your name?" He also held up a badge.

Al had forgotten that Randy was a chunk. At six foot five and about two hundred fifty pounds of gym-hardened muscle, the other guy had to look up at him. Randy had grown up tossing fifty-pound bales of hay onto a truck at his dad's spread and had added more bulk as he'd filled out as a man.

The guy hesitated a second or two. "Haskell. Eldridge Haskell. But folks call me Bean."

"What the hell's holding you up?" someone coming out of the low barn yelled.

"Just talking to these guys, Pa."

"What guys?"

"Deputies, so they say."

Bean's father lumbered around the front of the truck and approached quickly, in spite of a limp that suggested he'd fallen off something once and perhaps had not received the best medical care.

"Did you tell them to get off our property?"

"I did. They didn't."

The old man was winding up. His face flushed redder, and he sought to straighten his shoulders. He wore coveralls, too, but his had faded with wear until they were nearly grey.

Victor had stepped away and was talking on his phone.

"We'd like to take a look at those emus you're loading into the truck," Randy said.

"Well, you'll wait a long spell 'fore I let you do that."

"You're Jasp Haskell, aren't you?" Al asked.

"Used to be. Now I'm 'Old Man Jasp' to the neighbors, and a sad lot they are. But I can still hold my own." He glanced toward the ranch house as if measuring how far he would have to go to pull one of the long guns off a wall.

"Got it," Victor called out. "We have probable cause, and we have a warrant."

Jasp walked back toward the others.

A sudden move surprised Randy. Bean shot around him and raced toward the truck's cab, probably headed for the glove box. Al knew what he kept there.

"Halt!" Randy yelled.

Victor gave Al an eye roll at that.

As Bean shot past, Al dove and grabbed at both ankles, bringing them tightly together. All of Bean's momentum went into falling forward and slamming into the hard ground, with a little bounce of his head.

Al sprang back to his feet. Bean sat up slowly and looked around with a rattled glaze to his eyes.

"I think you'd best put him in the back seat for a spell until we have a look here," Victor told Randy.

Randy helped Bean to his feet and led him to the cruiser.

"Are we going to have any trouble with you?" Victor asked Jasp.

The senior Haskell shook his head. He nodded toward Al. "Hell, that guy's my age, and he done opened a can of whoop-ass on my boy there. I don't fancy a round of that."

Al didn't say anything. He would have grinned if his elbows weren't stinging and one knee wasn't sore. But he had to put on a front for the others.

Randy came back, and they all headed in the dark around to the back of the truck. Randy was carrying the case containing the pet-chip reader. "Thought we'd need this."

"Someone's got to get in that trailer with those birds and check for chips," Victor said, "and you know the rule about seniority." Victor stayed close to the old man, in case he decided to bolt.

Randy took the scanner out of its case. With it in one hand and a long-handled flashlight in the other, he slipped inside the trailer's back door when Al held it open.

Thumping and banging came from inside, followed by a muffled yell or two.

When Randy shot out the trailer's back door a few minutes later, his hair was mussed, one shirt sleeve was torn, and his eyes were open wide. "Those damn things sure tried to give me what for, but they're the stolen birds, all right."

Victor turned to Jasp, who just shrugged. He started to let Victor lead him to the cruiser to put in the back seat next to his son. But at the last second, some old fight-or-flee instinct kicked in, and he took off in a run toward the ranch house, scurrying like a crab trying to run straight. He'd barely gone a step or two before Randy caught him by the back of the coveralls and lifted him, carried him to the cruiser, and put him in.

Al reached up to give Randy a hearty pat on a hard shoulder. By morning, there wouldn't have been any evidence.

"Well, you've cracked your first case on your premiere outing," Victor said to Randy. "Did you learn anything?"

"Well, I expect next time I'll pack a helmet or a whip and a chair."

Victor was making the call for a deputy to come pick up the Haskells while Al eased over and leaned against the side of the truck. He was going to have a lump and a bruise or two, but it hadn't been his worst day of mentoring.

Whether from his dad being in the back seat beside him or from a sudden wash of shame, Bean decided to try to hammer and kick his way out of the back seat.

The two backup deputies in uniforms arrived just before Bean managed to break a window. As they took him to the back of their cruiser, he was still full of fight and broke loose.

As he went to rush past, Randy grabbed him by the coveralls, pulled him close, and twisted one arm until it was straight. He held Bean with one hand on his upper arm and the other twisting Bean's wrist, while shoving a thumb hard into the nerve center between Bean's thumb and forefinger. Bean tried to hit or kick at Randy, but Randy squeezed harder, and Bean stopped.

He went along, high onto his tiptoes and quietly, bold emu rustler though he was.

"You've got a good partner there, Victor," Al said, "at least for the physical stuff. You'd best hang onto him."

"We get some detecting skills into him, he'll do fine," Victor said. "Can't say much for the brain power of Bean there, waiting until he was outnumbered five to one before making his break for it."

"No, you can't count him as the brightest stick in the rhubarb patch," Al said.

"Well, the acorn didn't fall far from the tree. Emu rustling, of all things. There was a spell back a while ago where emu farmers were just setting them free. Even so, they don't fetch much." Victor shook his head as he moved toward their car. The other cruiser pulled away and was soon out of sight.

As far as Al was concerned, it had been a case of detection-lite, but he was glad enough to just head back to the department to do the usual pile of paperwork. Even when there was nothing mysterious or too complex, the messing about with reports took hours.

?

Dawn was oozing across the horizon like an orange-pink broken egg. Al felt tired all the way to the toes of his boots. Each foot felt like a bag of sand. One knee was throbbing, and he could feel an abrasion or two scabbing over. He pulled his truck into the parking lot of a place called Madrigal Joe's Coffee Shop, where he and Fergie had done a few stakeouts, met offline with the sheriff department's techno wizard, Meat Jenkins, and just had coffee. That was what he needed right now—a really good cup of coffee.

He dragged along feet that felt like two deflated tires.

At the early hour, only a half dozen people were in the coffee shop, and only one was ahead of him in line to get a cup. As much as needing a good cup of coffee after a Styrofoam cup or two of burnt-oil-tasting sludge at the sheriff's department, he wanted to feel a familiar place around him.

Normally, he looked around and spoke to others, but he sought to stand up straight and not let his shoulders slump. He kept his eyes on the barista as he whipped a double-foam latte for the guy ahead of Al.

He felt flat, washed out, and unsatisfied somehow. Sure, it had been a quick fix. The problem had been stolen farm animals, and they had solved it quickly and with a minimum of fuss—that is, if he didn't count Bean thrashing at the end. But it still hadn't felt right, and he wasn't sure what he was missing. Maybe it came down to how much knowledge he had imparted. He shook it off. He was probably just tired and a tiny bit grumpy.

Once he had his black coffee in hand, he turned and started for the door. Then he saw her in the corner at a table, talking intently with a man. He blinked. Yep, that was Fergie.

He realized he'd stopped walking. The man, who looked ten, maybe twenty years younger than Al and had thick dark hair, had his eyes fixed on Fergie's. Al made himself take another step and keep moving, wondering if he should just go over to the table and say hi.

Then Fergie bent closer and reached to put her hand over the back of the man's hand for a moment before removing it.

Al kept moving. He walked out the door and across the parking lot then climbed into his truck. For a minute, he just sat there. Then he started the truck and headed for his home, where he'd been expecting to see Fergie waiting.

Chapter Two

Al pulled up in front of his house and sat there a moment. Fergie's car wasn't in its usual place, of course. He didn't feel like going in.

Finally, ten minutes later, he got out. So early in the morning, Bonnie and Maury might not even be up.

Al didn't know when he'd felt so out of sorts, so tired but not wanting to go inside and go to bed.

He got out of the truck slowly, went to the front door, and opened it. He could hear Maury and Bonnie futzing around downstairs. Tanner came running to the door. Al reached for the leash beside the door, hooked up his eager dog, and stayed outside. He went around the house and down the hill to the level below.

Tanner trotted along beside him, glad at the chance for an outing.

At the dock, he turned left and went to the boat shed, hit the switch, and lowered the boat so he and Tanner could get in. His rods and tackle box were there, as were the couple of rods he'd gotten Fergie. It would be the first time she hadn't gone along on one of his recent fishing outings.

He lifted Tanner into the boat, got in himself, then lowered the boat the rest of the way until it bobbed on the water's surface.

The water was like glass, and mist rose off the surface in clouds that obscured some of the shoreline. He didn't go fast, not wanting to kick up a wake. Tanner crowded close, pressing his side against Al's leg. Al couldn't see another boat on the water in any direction.

The last time he and Fergie had been out on the water, they had gotten into a nice run of largemouth bass along a cliff that marked one side of the shore leading back into Cow Creek. They had gotten a hit on about every third cast for the whole stretch. A school of good-sized fish had been fixed there, whether from bait fish being present or from scouting for spawning beds in the weeks to come.

He pulled the boat up close to that wall of limestone, pocked by holes that served as bird nests and moss-covered doorways for lizard homes.

He sat there with one hand on Tanner, patting and rubbing the dog's soft fur. When the boat started to drift too close to the cliff, he dropped the electric motor in and eased the boat away, but he didn't pick up a rod. He sat on the front seat and looked out across the water.

Other boats finally began to stir along the shorelines. Some kicked up froth as they towed water skiers. A few Jet Skis added their noise and their riders' waving arms to the brightening day.

Tanner climbed up onto the front deck and eased closer until he could lay his head across Al's foot.

The sun was at its zenith when Al finally shook his head. He stood, brought the electric motor in, and climbed back into the driver's seat. He hadn't cast a single lure.

On the way back to the house, he tried to think about what he might say. He had been with Fergie for something like three years. *Had it been that long? Or longer?*

He'd never been jealous before, but she hadn't mentioned a meeting with anyone.

Maybe I'm just... Well, hell, I didn't know what I am or what I'm not.

They hadn't really talked about it much—his fault, probably—but when a man was around a woman that long, it usually led to something. He hadn't made the move to a more serious level, if that was the way it was described those days. He'd just been plodding along, taking each day as it came, while Maury, once a dreaded horndog of a brother, had of all things settled down, gotten married, and even had a baby. It couldn't make Fergie feel too good that Al was just there, nothing more.

By the time Al could see his house ahead and had slowed the boat, his mind was a whirl of unrelated and certainly unproductive thoughts. He could see a figure sitting in one of the Adirondack chairs on the dock. He could tell it was Fergie as he got closer.

Tanner got up on the front deck and began wagging his tail.

"No fish?" she called as he eased the boat into its slip and raised the hoist until it caught.

"Nope. No fish." He lifted Tanner out, and the dog shot across to Fergie.

"Are you in a pout?" Fergie asked.

"What?"

"I *am* a detective. There's a to-go coffee cup from Madrigal Joe's Coffee Shop in your truck's beverage holder. You took off like a shot, didn't speak to Maury or Bonnie, and haven't been to bed yet. You must be tired and a little befuddled is my guess."

"Well, I... I guess I am a bit."

Her mouth tugged into an ironic twist at one corner, what he'd heard called a *moue*. "As much as I'd enjoy stringing you on some to see you twist and turn, revealing that you do have an emotional core, I'm going to let you down easy, since I need to go away for a while to help someone."

"The guy you were talking to?"

"Yeah. You know, I could keep you squirming. But one of the things I value in the way we get along is that we tend to shoot straight with each other. We don't talk a lot or too much, but we usually are candid and clear."

"Are we easing up to the candid part soon?"

"I'll tell you if you tell me how you spent your night."

"I was out chasing giant chickens."

She pursed her lips, and her brow furrowed.

"Emus," he said. "We had to find and wrangle in a couple of emu rustlers. Wasn't as easy as it sounds, though the birds weren't much of a flight risk."

"Well, if you're going to just make stuff up... oh, never mind. The guy you saw me with was someone I used to date long ago, in my past."

"Did you know him pretty well?"

"Pretty well." She looked like either she'd just swallowed gum she wasn't chewing or she was suppressing a smile. "Oh, come on. You're not jealous, are you?"

"What did he want?"

"He wanted me to come help him with something urgent. I think I'm going to do it."

"What is this something?"

"His stepson, Baron Fieldings, has gone missing."

"Really? He must be a young man. Are you sure he didn't just take a powder to sow some oats or seek a thrill?"

"He's thirty-two and still lives at home with his mom, who Colin only married a year ago, when she became a widow."

"Stepping right up to the plate, your friend Colin."

"Let's stay focused on the boy here."

"Young man."

"If you insist." Fergie took a deep breath. "It's not like him to just take off."

"Did they file a missing person report?"

"Yeah. But they don't care much for the sheriff. She's a woman, by the way."

"Really. Is she the kind of sheriff to get one of her retired detectives to come in and chase over hell's half acre after emus?"

"That's really what you were doing?"

"I'm afraid so, as much as you perhaps envisioned something slightly more glamorous. But don't think there wasn't danger. A ticked-off emu is nothing to scoff at."

When she didn't say anything, he asked, "This Colin guy, he's really married, right?"

"Yeah." She chuckled. "I suspected not knowing that was part of what was making you twitchy. There's a chance you might even know his wife. She's our age, even went to the same school, was in the same class. She and her sister were the McCampbell twins, Meryl and Ferrill."

"I remember hearing something about one of them."

"Well, he—Colin Tansey, the one you saw me with—is married to the good one."

"Is he nearly our age as well? He didn't look it."

"Nevertheless, he is. Well-preserved and fit but only two years younger than the twin he married."

"A twin who is our age." Al huffed. "You know, folks our age get to where they're apt to have a favorite chair. Some like to go on about what ails them."

"You're not like that."

"Not yet. The day will come."

"All that aside, I aim to help Colin. Will you be okay here without me?"

"Really? You intend to do this on your own?"

"Don't you want an opportunity to miss me—I mean, if I go off on this alone?"

"Aren't we like Batman and Robin? How could you leave me behind?"

"But I would get to be Batman this time, wouldn't I?" she said.

"If you think the cape will fit you."

"You've been hogging that cape far too long now."

"Okay, though I've got to tell you, I was never a fan of Robin's tights."

"But you like mine." She pursed her lips. "What if I'd just gone away, said nothing?"

"That has a Zen answer. Even saying nothing is saying something. But you would have left a trail of bread crumbs or something. I'd have found you because you'd want me to."

"I'm glad it didn't come to that. I'll be glad to have you along on this."

He hesitated a moment, focusing on the sheen of the ripple the wind was kicking up across the lake's surface. "Now, about this Colin guy—"

"It was a while ago. A long while ago."

"Okay, then."

"We all have a past, especially at our ages."

"I'll tell you something I learned from sitting many hours alone, bobbing gently on the water in my fishing boat. You can spend way too much time stewing over regrets, mistakes, and things you should have done or not done. It's best to leave all that back there where it belongs. There's nothing you can do about any of it, anyway."

"There's only one thing I'd like to know," she said with a tiny edge to her words. "Did you just stumble into that coffee shop at that hour, or were you in any way spying on me?"

He shook his head. "Just some of the usual sad serendipity life enjoys dishing up."

"You shouldn't have felt sad."

"Right. Like you said, it was a long time ago."

"And, as you so aptly put it, sometimes it's best not to look back too hard."

Chapter Three

"Do you know what I like about fishing?" He glanced over at Fergie.

Her hands were on the ten and two position on the steering wheel, usually a sign she was thinking deeply. "What? That you wouldn't have to be along on this cockamamie mission as my wingman?" The corner of her mouth tugged up a bit as she said it.

"I was thinking of the calm of being on the water, watching the birds, and feeling the breeze, even if I happen to be fishing in empty water."

"Or mooning over your girlfriend possibly having a lover."

"Your words, not mine. Anyway, what makes you think that?"

"Oh, come on, Al, do you wish to toss aside this fragile thing we have called understanding?"

"Speaking of which, you took a while saying goodbye to the baby and his parents, Bonnie and Maury. We would have been on the road an hour earlier."

"And you took as much time saying goodbye to your fur pal, Tanner."

"Okay. We're even. I guess we both have to admit to having something like a family."

He stayed quiet for a few miles after that, listening to the hum of asphalt beneath their wheels and taking in the passing country around them. A number of motorcycles, pickups, and RVs passed them going either way. He looked around more than usual. Though he'd been on the highway a number of times, as a passenger, he seemed to see more. The traffic seemed hurried, worried, and perhaps on the edge of chaos.

Each stretch of road had a slightly alien feel to it, and not just because Fergie was driving.

They left the six-lane road for a four-lane one and eventually ended up on a two-lane one. He saw cattle, horses, and even a couple of llamas and a zebra, but no emus.

He had a general idea that they were heading somewhere toward Houston, but the destination could easily be nearer the Upper Rio Grande Valley, out in the wide-open spaces that still existed in Texas. The state may have had a few of the largest metropolitan areas in the nation, but it was still possible to find large chunks of Bumfart Nowhere, and they seemed to be headed there. He left the leadership of the outing to Fergie, and she seemed to be enjoying that.

"We're going to arrive at or after dinner time," he said, "so maybe we'd better grab a bite before we get there."

"And just like that, I see a cozy-looking diner up ahead. You know, you're not as hard to understand or anticipate as you think, Al."

She parked in an open spot between a couple of pickups and a Harley, and they got out.

Al stretched his back and swiveled at his waist a couple of times before they went in. As he walked along the aisle between a row of red-and-white booths and a counter row of stools, he smelled fried chicken, onion rings, and burgers done the rich, fatty, tasty way.

In spite of the number of vehicles outside, only one guy sat at the counter, with a plate and a white ceramic mug of coffee in front of him. The guy raised his head from the plate that contained what looked like a half-eaten grilled cheese sandwich. With his head tilted back, he gave Al a glare that suggested supreme overconfidence to the point of animal arrogance.

Al and Fergie eased into a booth midway down the row, where they could look out the window and see Fergie's car.

The counterman scraped at a huge griddle with a wide silver spatula. He glanced at Al, at the restroom door, then back at Al.

The lone waitress raised an eyebrow and started bustling in their direction. She came to an abrupt halt when the man sitting at the counter rose and started toward the booth where Al and Fergie sat.

"What you doin'? I was sittin' there," the man said, coming to the end of the table and looking down at them. "My friends and I were there." He glanced toward the men's-room door. Al knew his courage came from whoever was back there.

Al figured the guy for five foot six or thereabouts. He spoke with his chin raised, the way Mussolini did in old newsreels.

All the booths around them were empty. Fergie started to say something. Al reached out and grabbed her forearm. The smaller man stepped aside as Al helped her get to her feet, all six foot two of her. The guy had to look up at her. Al and Fergie headed for the front door, not quickly but not letting any dust settle on them either.

He caught the worried stare of the waitress and the mixture of concern and relief on the face of the man behind the counter, who shrugged as if to say, "What can you do?" Al was glad they were getting out of harm's way, but the waitress and the counterman were stuck there.

As soon as they were outside, Fergie spoke first. "I recall a time when you would have knocked the eyebrows off a fellow like that for a whole lot less."

Al didn't say anything, just walked briskly toward her car.

"I know," Fergie said. "He's a problem, but he's someone else's problem right now. You and I are on a mission elsewhere."

"You know what's going on here, don't you?" Al stood outside the passenger door, waiting.

"Yeah," Fergie said. "I saw it too. The tattoo on that guy's forearm. I'm just surprised his whole face and neck weren't covered in tattoos."

Al had seen that sort of arrogant look before. It was almost common among those who wore similar tattoos. "We're a good hundred miles from Houston but not far from the ranch where we're headed. I hope this is an awkward coincidence and means nothing."

"And he wasn't by himself, or he might not have been so full of hot air." Fergie opened her car, and they climbed in it. "I would expect to see that sort of thing in one of the big cities but not way out here. The world's population is sure growing and creeping out into all available spaces."

Al popped open the glove box. His Sig Sauer was in there with her Glock. To keep them from clanking around, he'd put his pistol into an old sock. He took it out of the sock and jacked a shell into the chamber. "He was wearing blue and white with a blue bandana. That's what made me look for the tat." Blue and white were also the colors on the flag of El Salvador.

"What are you going to do? I thought this was someone else's problem."

"Not really. You saw the looks on the faces of the waitress and counterman. They were being more than bullied—they were being terrorized, and the fear showed. That guy's on the prowl for a fight, and I intend to give him the chance for one."

"You can't go around saving the world, Al."

"No, but I can adjust one little piece at a time." He started to open his door.

"Wait. You know how active law enforcement feels if someone charges into a diner, waving a gun around."

"I'll just have it along just in case, tucked inside my shirt at the back."

She reached out a hand and put it on his forearm to hold him in place. "Give it a second."

A state trooper's black-and-white cruiser whooshed into the gravel parking lot. While the driver was still getting out, another cruiser pulled in beside it.

"Whew," she said. "Looks like you don't have to slip on your Batman costume. One of them must have managed a call and let those troopers know they were being intimidated."

"Would you have felt okay leaving those diner workers to their fate?"

"No."

"I didn't think so."

"I'm just surprised you don't want to go back and help those guys in uniform."

"Fergie, I have yet to meet a DPS trooper who thinks he needs help from anyone, especially someone who is no longer official in any way." He slipped the gun back into its sock and put it back in the glove box. "I just wonder what those gangbanger thugs were doing way out here, so far from a city."

"Soon, there won't be any country anymore, if these guys are spreading into it." She started the car and turned out of the diner's lot, glancing into her rearview mirror.

Al turned to look back at the diner as they pulled away. He supposed a couple of troopers would be enough to dampen what had almost been going on back there. In the past, he probably would have gone back to help them. Maybe he *was* getting older. Or just smarter.

"The Mara Salvatrucha," she said. "MS-13."

The tattoo Al had seen was of the gang's hand signs. Gangs like the Bloods, the Crips, the Latin Kings, and the Sureños all had them. They called them "stacks." The one for the Mara Salvatrucha was the thumb holding down the middle two fingers with the forefinger and little finger extended. "You probably saw more of these guys in the city than we did out in the county."

"They were a spotty presence in Austin and more or less got the boot from Tango Blast and a few other cartel-related gangs. They're much bigger in San Antonio and Houston." Fergie's hands tightened on the wheel. "When we first came across them, some of our guys thought MS-13 had appropriated the hand sign for the University of Texas. Except the Salvadorans weren't going for a Texas long-horn—they meant the far more satanic devil's horns. When they hold it upside down it forms an M for MS-13 or simply Maras."

"We didn't have a major problem with them in the county," Al said. "But when we did, it was worse than dealing with Colombians wearing spurs. Most of the victims we came across were teenagers, fifteen or sixteen, and they'd not only been stabbed but mutilated. One sixteen-year-old boy had been shot twenty-five times, and two fifteen-year-old girls were chopped up pretty good with a machete. But whoever caught up with the Salvadorans before we found them did as good a job of cutting them up until we could barely make out the tattoos, and these guys had been covered with them, from the tops of their shaved heads to their toes."

"You get a motto of *mata, viola, controla*—kill, rape, control—and you have to live up to it with truly shocking acts of violence designed to instill fear, including gang rape and human trafficking." Fergie shook her head.

"The fried chicken in that diner sure smelled good. But until we know that spotting a lone *chequeo* and possibly a couple of pals in the head is just a coincidence and has nothing to do with this missing person we're supposed to be helping with, I'm all for steering clear of the type. It's just damned odd bumping into that sort way the hell out here, so far from a big city."

"You think the one crowding our booth was at the lowest rung, a *chequeo*, because he's not yet covered from stem to stern in tattoos?"

"Exactly. He's probably survived his initiation beatdown, but he's about a gallon of tattoo ink short of being a high-ranking member of his *clica*. He makes up for that with attitude."

Fergie's frown took on a firm set. "I can recall when these MS-13 guys weren't a Texas problem at all. I heard about them out in California and over on the East Coast, but I doubt if there were ten thousand of them in all of the U.S. I'm no expert on how to handle such gangs, but it seems all of them who got deported back to El Salvador got even tougher and higher up as they regrouped and were recruited by the Sinaloa cartel and other cartels who were doing battle with Los Zetas. Nowadays, I've heard there are over a hundred thousand of them in America. I guess they have to spread out to somewhere. But I sure hope it isn't out here."

Al glanced at the road behind them. They were far enough away that he couldn't see anything. "I hate to let even the glimpse of one of those thugs keep me from a meal, but until we know more about what's going on out in these parts, I think we just need to take our learning curve slowly and avoid any unnecessary distractions."

"There's a taco truck up ahead. Want me to stop there?"

"You might as well. We should eat. It won't be fried chicken, but there you have it."

"You could always get a chicken taco."

"I was hoping for *carnitas*. You'll note I didn't say *lengua* in a hopeful sort of way."

"Wise choice. Go for the pork. As for you getting any tongue..." She let that hang there.

Al was content to savor a quiet moment or two as she pulled into the gravel by the taco truck.

It could have been the beginning of dusk setting in, but the afternoon had taken on a dimmer cast. A shadow seemed to creep across the day in a way that Al couldn't see as a good omen at all.

Chapter Four

The sky had darkened until Fergie needed her headlights to stay on the sparsely graveled twin ruts of the lane that led to the ranch house that had been out of sight from the road.

She pulled up at the front door. Before she could turn the engine off, Colin came hustling out to wave for her to park closer to the two-car garage.

As she climbed out, he said, "I've got a place for you up there." He pointed toward an apartment over the garage.

When Al climbed out the passenger-side door, Colin's eyes opened wider. "Oh."

Al stepped closer and held out a hand. Up close, Colin didn't seem quite the threat he had seemed earlier. He was Al's height and was handsome enough, but his smile was weak and uncertain. "How long have you had this ranch?"

"Meryl bought the place just five years ago. It was always a kind of dream of hers. I married her a year ago, and... here we are." He waved a hand around the expansive dark around them then turned to Al. "I know about you, followed you in the media. You were a hotshot detective with the sheriff's department, and you were in the same class as my wife, Meryl."

"I thought you married Ferrill, the other twin?" Al glanced toward Fergie. She was shaking her head.

"I did. That was my first wife. She died. Horrible car accident. Meryl's husband had passed on too. Heart attack. So... here we are." Colin didn't sound quite so proud or certain about that. "It's her son,

Baron, who has come up missing. I'm glad you're both here to help with that."

Al felt about as comfortable as he might have had he stepped into one of the nearby cow pies he was pretty sure he could smell without having to see.

The glance Colin gave Fergie said he wished she had come alone. That somehow turned Al around and made him glad he'd come along.

"Is there anything we should be doing tonight?" Fergie asked.

Colin shook his head. "I just got a call from the sheriff's office that they haven't turned up anything. I'll see that you get a look around the spread first thing in the morning. We're still scratching our heads and hoping for the best. I was starting to get desperate, which is why I reached out to Fergie."

Al and Fergie's eyes clicked for a second. She was probably wondering, as he was, why they hadn't been taken to meet Meryl, their former classmate.

"Did he take anything with him, luggage, stuff like that?"

"No. His truck's here in the garage, and all his clothing is still in his room, the way he left it. He was here one minute, and poof, gone the next."

As Colin led them up the wooden steps to the garage apartment, Al asked, "Are you mostly into cattle?"

"Oh my, no. I don't have the hands for that. I have a few hundred head but nothing like the big boys. I'm mostly in hay here. It grows, we harvest it, and it sells for a lot more than you'd think. I help run the place, but it's hers, and Meryl's by no means clear on the place yet but got it with part of what she got from her husband's death."

"From the insurance?" Fergie asked.

"That and selling off her property, a pretty upscale house in Houston, near enough to the heart of things to see theater plays and symphonies. There are times I think she misses all that. But the air is sure better out here. I had a condo that I've since sold."

He swung the door open at the top of the stairs, and Al recognized Wes Sharmée at once. He was another former classmate of theirs, one who Al heard had struggled through some difficult times after doing his time overseas. He was still lanky and tall, but his face was heavily lined now, and when he looked up, a hole showed where his front four upper teeth should have been. "I'll be outta here soon as I can, Colin. I'm a-hustling."

Wes paused for a second. "Well, I'll be. Fergie and Al. I haven't seen you two in a crippled coon's age or two. I heard you were both in some kind of law or other. Are you an item now?"

"Are we putting you out of your room?" Al glanced around. The twin-sized bed was centered in the sparsely furnished room. He could see a cramped toilet and shower inside the open door in the far corner. A two-burner hot plate sat on a folding table set up under the pulled drapes of window on the other side of the room.

Fergie was staring at the twin bed.

Al nearly chuckled, imagining her feet sticking out of one end of it. The bed was probably long enough, but it was damned narrow. It was going to be one interesting night.

"Look, we hate to put you out of your room," Fergie said.

"No worries. I'm used to being shuttled about. There'll be a cot in the bunkhouse I can use. I can put up with Ike's snoring one more night. It won't kill me."

"Is Ike one of the hands?"

"No, Ike's a dog. Big ol' yella lab. The only other hand is Bo Melford. He hardly snores at all, compared to the dog."

"One big happy family," Al muttered.

"I s'pose you two will be fine in that bed." Wes was suppressing what was probably a smirk. "I guess you could spoon or something."

"Al's more of the fork type," Fergie said.

Wes looked puzzled then seemed to get it. Darned if he didn't blush a bit. He glanced toward Colin, who shook his head. The two of them left the room and headed down the stairs.

As Al undressed, Fergie could see the large bruise on one knee and scabs forming on his elbow and forearm. "Oh my," she said. "I thought I detected a tiny limp to your step, one you were trying not to show."

"Emu wrangling's a young man's game, Fergie. What else can I tell you?"

They finally managed to squeeze onto the small bed, and spooning was about the only way to do that. Both were putting off too much heat, so Al stayed outside the sheet, wearing just his shirt and briefs.

"Are you awake?" he whispered.

"Yes."

"Have you ever thought much about identical twins?"

"I mean, when we were in school, I used to wonder about the boys who would date Meryl and Ferrill. They both looked identical. What difference could it make to date one or the other?"

"I heard, as you probably did, too, that one of them was kind of bad," she said.

"Like an evil twin?"

"Not *like* one. *Exactly* an evil twin. She got into trouble any number of times. The McCampbell twins were kind of notorious for that."

"Yet they looked exactly alike."

"And here's the bigger deal. Colin married them both, one after the other."

"Didn't you say he's married to the good twin now?"

"He'd better hope so."

Fergie's words were fading, and soon, she was asleep. In time, though not as quickly as Fergie, so was he.

He woke from a fragile sleep to hear crackling pops.

"Is that what I think it is?" Fergie asked.

"I fear so." Al slid out of bed and went to pull the drape aside and look out the window. "I can't see anything, but that sure enough sounds like gunfire and plenty of it. What time is it?"

"Three a.m. I wonder if anyone in the house is awake from this."

"I'm going to find out." Al pulled on his pants and boots then went out the door and down the stairs.

He looked for a flashlight beam moving around or any indication anyone was stirring. At first, it looked like he was the only one up. As he circled around to the back of the ranch house, he could see someone standing in silhouette against the sky. He drew closer and could make out Colin in a bathrobe and slippers, staring off in the direction of the noise.

Al made a little scraping sound with his boot steps as he got closer.

Without turning his way, Colin said, "Damn fools."

"Who's doing that?" Al asked.

"Neighbors. They're just exuberant. Burning off steam, the sheriff tells me."

"Who lives over there?"

"I don't know. Some guy from Mexico bought the land earlier this year."

"Do you think whoever's over there has anything to do with the Mara Salvatrucha?"

Al couldn't see Colin shudder, but his voice had a quiver to it. "I surely as hell hope not. Do you like ants? I mean the kind that swarm all over you and bite and bite. Well, that's what the Maras are named after, the sort of ants that swarm and devour everything in their path."

"Do you think whoever is over there has any ties to your stepson's disappearance?"

"I have no way of knowing. It's why I asked Fergie to come have a look."

"The sheriff doesn't think so?"

"She says not."

"She?" Al knew that but listened for Colin's response.

Colin nodded. "And she's Latina too."

"Does that make her sympathetic to cartel-linked gangs?"

"I certainly hope not."

"What do you want us to do?" Al asked.

"In the morning, you can take a look around the spread here. That's where he went missing. His horse came back without him."

"The sheriff's men looked around?"

"And didn't find anything, they said."

"This sheriff, she's not in any way friends with your neighbors, is she?" Al tried again.

"I don't know. I don't know any damned thing." Exasperation was showing in Colin's voice. "I just hope you can help. Heaven knows we're getting no help around here."

Al could have said something about how difficult it might turn out to be if they found the sheriff to be in any way corrupt. Where cartels were involved, the bribes could be in the millions. But he kept his mouth shut about that. Al reminded himself that these were early times.

The shooting stopped abruptly and didn't start up again.

"Probably ran out of ammo," Al said.

"Until tomorrow," Colin said.

"Until then."

Chapter Five

Before the sun rose, Al and Fergie got up and took turns in the tiny shower. While Fergie showered, Al walked around in the small garage apartment, loosening up his bruised knee, which had stiffened some in the night.

When she came out of the shower, wrapped in a towel that was wearing into tatters on one end, she saw him limping about.

"Don't ever get old," he said.

"Gotcha. That shower ought to invigorate you. It's mostly cold."

He hurried into the bathroom.

He was shivering by the time his short shower was over. He reached for a towel and found none. Fergie stood in the doorway, holding out the damp towel she had used. "Welcome to the Ritz Carleton."

When they both went down the stairs and crossed over to the ranch house, the sun was just bursting yellow and orange up from the horizon.

Al tried the front door and found it locked. "That's odd."

Fergie reached for the cord that hung from the tongue of a bell to the right of the door.

"Let's just go around," Al said. He led the way around the house and to a wide flagstone patio with a stone grill at one end.

They went to the back door. Al opened it, and they went inside, right into a large kitchen. The lights were on, but the room was empty, the table cleared.

Al looked at Fergie. Her mouth was slightly open as she looked around. Large silver appliances and granite countertops lined one wall.

A pair of sinks stretched beneath a picture window that looked out onto the patio. The walls were all done in knotty pine.

"Do not do the despair, *señor* and *señora*." A tiny Latina woman emerged from what looked like a walk-in pantry. She put the bottle of hot sauce she carried onto the table and got a bowl of salsa out of the fridge. She hustled over to the oven and took out a warmer full of tortillas and a plate covered in foil, which she whisked off. The plate held scrambled eggs and meat.

Fergie leaned closer. "*Lengua?*"

"*Sí.* I have *café* for you as well."

"And it's *señorita,*" Fergie said.

The woman tilted her head back to look up at Fergie. "*Sí, señorita.* I am called Gaby."

"Gaby is short for Gabriella." The voice came from the doorway, where a young towheaded girl came into the kitchen from the house. "Hi. I'm Cricket. I'm eleven. I'd be in the sixth grade if I went to school. But I'm being homeschooled by my Auntie Gran."

"How's that going?" Fergie sat down at the table.

"Well, I know my algebras up to G, H, I." Cricket pulled out a chair and plopped into it to watch them eat.

"What?"

"Oh, I'm just joshing you. It's been a while since we had company, and it's always jolly fun, except my Auntie Gran isn't in the best mood."

"I suppose you mean Meryl. Speaking of which, where is she?"

"They had to ride out early. One of the hands came across something."

"This is Fergie"—Al swept a hand toward her—"and I'm Al." He reached out a hand.

Cricket shook it and grinned when he went to shake Gaby's hand and she backed away. "She's not used to that sort of thing."

Gaby poured coffee into two brown mugs and brought them to the table.

"Are you going to join us?" Al saw that only two places had been set as he sat down.

"I ate a while back. But I'll sit a spell until we saddle up. Which one of you has ridden a horse the least?"

"That would be me." Al held up a hand.

"Then we'll saddle Ol' Sal for you. She's a mare almost anyone could ride. I learned to ride on her myself once, ages ago."

Fergie raised her eyebrows at the girl. "You seem pretty chipper for someone whose father is missing."

"Oh, I try." She showed a pair of dimples with her grin. "He's gone missing before and has always showed up. We might as well ride out and see what the to-do is all about." She gave the outside they could see through the window a worried glance. "You're here to help find my dad, aren't you? I really am beginning to fret a little. Being gone this long isn't like him."

When Al reached for the hot sauce, Cricket happily clapped her hands. "I like people who like hot sauce. It means you're peppy like me."

Of course, that meant Fergie had to slather some of the hot sauce on her salsa, although she didn't have the iron stomach Al did.

Full of breakfast tacos and coffee, Al and Fergie followed Cricket out to the stables.

"You said you learned to ride on Ol' Sal here," Al said as he helped put the saddle on the mare.

"Yeah. This spread used to be my dad's, but he got into money troubles, and we were lucky that Auntie Gran had just come into money."

Al couldn't help but delight at her innocent candor, spilling all about her family. He wanted to ask her what happened to her mother but figured she would get around to saying something about that in time. "Are you going to ride that black stallion? What's his name?"

"Diablo, of course. What else could it be?"

They saddled up a roan gelding named Bob for Fergie. Then they swung up into their saddles and headed out across the spread. They rode in the pastures where cattle grazed. To their left, hay fields that were going to be ready to be baled soon spread out in golden waves.

In a surprisingly short while, Al could turn in his saddle and no longer see the ranch house. The hills rolled as they veered farther right between grazing groups of cattle. Al had heard that running a spread wasn't all fun and profits, that surprises brought along years when much more money went out than came in. A lot of the ranches within a commutable drive to the big cities had been gobbled up and turned into suburban-style developments. He'd have hated to see that happen to Meryl's place. Its saving grace was that it was probably too far from any city for that.

Al glanced toward Fergie and got a grin in return. She seemed to be quite enjoying herself, bouncing along on Bob.

The rising sun was to their left, so they were heading south. Al saw Cricket lean from one side to the other in her saddle and figured out she was following something. When he looked hard at the ground, he could see faint hoofprints.

Someone had cleared out the scrub and patches of prickly pear cactus with a Bobcat, but the growth was starting to come back. Here and there, patches of chaparral filled an arroyo, a steep-sided gully cut into the ground by running water, often during the flash floods between dry spells. No sense in chewing themselves up by riding through them without chaps on. They rode around those, as well as any clusters of rocks that could conceal a rattlesnake.

Ahead, two horses were tied to low brush that looked like the start of a mesquite tree. A couple of figures stood nearby, not far from a fence line along the edge of the spread. A rough dirt road ran along the inside of the fence so the barrier could be routinely checked and maintained.

Al heard a vehicle coming before he saw it. A sheriff's department cruiser came bouncing and jostling along on the dirt road, kicking up quite a cloud of brown dust behind it.

"I wonder if they have news about your father," Fergie said.

"I hope so." Cricket gave Diablo a nudge with her heels, and he shot ahead.

As soon as she was out of hearing range, Fergie said, "She's such a chipper little thing. It hasn't occurred to her that any news a deputy brings might not be good."

"It will." Al gave Ol' Sal a nudge but got only a reluctant canter instead of a gallop. Fergie, riding Bob, easily passed him.

As he got closer, Al could make out Colin. The woman beside him was probably Meryl, though he hadn't seen her since high school. They stood over a body on the ground. His stomach lurched, thinking of little Cricket galloping eagerly that way.

Cricket had already dismounted by the time he and Fergie got to the little group. They got off and tied their horses to the same bit of brush.

Colin moved to one side, nearer the cruiser that had stopped. Al saw that the body on the ground was that of a calf. Relief swept through him.

From the sheriff's department cruiser, a stocky woman and a towering man came their way.

"You called me out here for this?" The woman looked down at the partially butchered calf.

"There was heavy shooting over yonder in the night." Colin nodded toward the ranch on the other side of the fence.

"You know as well as I do that it's not illegal to discharge firearms on your own property. Now, if you're hunting out of season and get caught by the fish-and-wildlife folks, that's another thing altogether and still none of *my* business."

"Someone took just the ribs on this side and the liver," Al said. "That's the way Native Americans used to do it. Raw hunger and daily needs drove that."

The woman squinted at him.

"This is Al Quinn and his friend Ferguson—Fergie—Jergens. They're both former law." Colin turned to Al and Fergie. "This is Rosa del Flores-Mendez. She's the sheriff of this county."

She kept her eyes fixed on Al. "Former law means current nobody."

"I'm just suggesting someone might've done it out of hunger. You have a missing man here, don't you?"

"I asked Fergie to come here and help find Meryl's son." For a moment, Colin looked like a worm squirming on a hook. "Al came along in the bargain. He was a sheriff's department detective once. She was an Austin city police detective."

"Here about Baron being missing, are you?" She looked up at her deputy. "You hear that, Took?"

The tall guy nodded. He looked the sort who was along to lift things like the back ends of cars and such.

"Looks like we made a trip out here for nothing." She looked down in disgust at the calf. Flies were buzzing around the raw red flesh. When she looked back up at Al, she said, "You've done missing persons before. What steps would you take?"

"I'd check the hospitals, morgue, and any place where he could stay with friends."

"Did all that."

"I'd check his cell phone and his bank accounts. Maybe see if he sold anything lately for cash."

"Did all that too." She frowned. "Is that all you got, bright boy?"

Al glanced toward Fergie. "We just got here. Once we've looked around a bit, we may know more."

"Well, you just look all you want, but don't get in my way. For all I know, Baron is dead and buried out any old where and never will be found. C'mon, Took." As she headed back toward the cruiser, she muttered, "I'm way smarter than those two will ever be."

Al spun in time to see tears stream down Cricket's small round face. She turned and ran toward her horse. She jerked the reins from the limb and climbed up into the saddle. Diablo took off at a hard gallop.

"That sheriff may think she's a smart one," Fergie said, "but she could stand a lesson or two in tact."

Chapter Six

"**I** wonder why a busy sheriff like her would come all the way out here to have a look at a dead calf," Al said. The cloud of dust was slowly settling, the cruiser out of sight.

Colin took off his straw cowboy hat and rubbed at the red line it had made across his forehead. "I just called in to the department about the calf. I didn't expect her to come traipsing out here."

"In fairness, the whole area has been under some tension lately. Baron having gone missing is only part of that," Meryl said. "But he's the most important part to me, of course."

Al hadn't really had a chance to look at her closely, but when he did, he blinked and looked closer. Both Meryl and Ferrill had been attractive identical twins in high school, but zow—Meryl looked like a woman in her early thirties, maybe even late twenties. He'd seen neither twin in many years, since he'd skipped the class reunions, so the way she looked rocked him back on his heels. He was just wondering if Ferrill had also managed to retain the same youthful appearance when he looked at Fergie and caught her frowning at him.

"I really appreciate you coming out, Fergie. I feel like any efforts to find him have been half-hearted at best." Meryl turned to Al. "And you are a bonus. I recall reading an article or two in the papers about some of your feats of detection. For the first time, I feel like we're in safe hands." She reached out and put a hand on Al's arm.

Al felt a tingle of electricity shoot up his arm and pop in a small explosion in his head, or at least it seemed that way until he caught a glance from Fergie. Her eyes had narrowed to slits. He took a step back.

"I'd better go see to Cricket," Meryl said. "She looked pretty upset, for her." She stepped away from them, swung herself up into the saddle of her horse, and soon had it trotting toward the ranch house.

"Isn't she something?" Colin said.

"She sure is," Fergie said. Her teeth were together, but she managed a smile when she turned to Colin. "How did she come to own a ranch way out here?"

Colin seemed to fixate on the flies beginning to swarm the open flesh of the dead calf. A flap of wings made him look up. The first of the buzzards, a turkey buzzard, had come to roost on the fence. "I guess that's important to know, though I don't think it has any bearing on Baron being missing."

"Let us decide," Fergie said.

"It's as simple as this. The spread here should have been doing fine, but Baron managed to get himself in trouble. He was going to lose the ranch. Meryl had just lost her husband and had gotten five hundred thousand in insurance money from his death. She bought the place, bailed Baron out of that mess. We haven't talked about all of their past, but I suspect she'd bailed him out a time or two before. He'd had a horrible marriage. His wife left him and didn't want custody of Cricket or even anything to do with her."

"Cricket seems pretty perky most of the time."

"Hardy resilience is all I can tell you."

The grazing cattle in the rest of the pasture were going about their business of eating grass. But they didn't move closer, as some cattle would. Al figured that might have to do with the dead calf, but as long as he'd covered the legal ups and downs as well as ins and outs of Travis County, he'd never become any kind of expert on cattle ranching.

"I don't understand," Fergie said. "The ranch could have been profitable, but suddenly it wasn't?"

"I guess that does beg an explanation." Colin reached up to run a finger along under his lower lip.

"It sure does." Fergie looked across the pasture in the direction Meryl had ridden.

Colin glanced around. He looked like he was searching for a place to sit. Al hoped the story wasn't going to take that long.

One of the horses nickered, and the others joined in. They had just spotted more buzzards arriving.

"The thing was, the boy got impatient, we think. His ranch was slowly, steadily getting by, but just barely. We, Meryl and I, think he was looking for other revenue streams, though he denied it. Still, the evidence seemed to be against him. A routine helicopter flyover by the sheriff's department claimed to have spotted the different color that marks a marijuana patch. While the cruisers were still on the way to the spread, somebody set fire to the patch and burned it, but the fire spread to the hay fields and even parts of the pasture. Baron lost his crop and several head of cattle. The sheriff couldn't do anything, and Baron claimed innocence, but the shadow of suspicion hung over him. And worse, he took a financial dip he couldn't afford."

Fergie tilted her head a half inch. "So he would have gone under if Meryl hadn't just come into five hundred thousand from her husband's death?"

Colin nodded. "I wish I had insured Ferrill for as much. But her death tore me up pretty bad. I wasn't worried about money, then, just her loss."

Al was thinking that it was fortunate Ferrill had a recently widowed twin, one of those little twists of fate. That made him ponder again how very young and attractive Meryl looked. He saw Fergie giving him the beady eye. Maybe she had a hunch what was on his mind. So he headed for the horses, and they all three mounted and rode toward the ranch house.

?

They dismounted outside the stable and walked the horses in through the open double doors. The inside was dark in the corners and far cooler than the heat outside.

Their former classmate Wes Sharmée came ambling out from a door at the end of the stables. Al figured the door led into a small bunkhouse just big enough for a couple of cots and a small bathroom. Wes was certainly not living the dream.

He smiled at them, and the big gap where teeth should have been drew Al's eye.

Colin handed his reins to Wes and walked back out of the stable, mumbling about doing something at the house.

Wes removed the saddle and other tack. He put the saddle on a wooden horse next to other saddles and hung everything else on a row of wooden pegs along the wall across from a row of stalls. Then he led the horse out to a corral and turned it loose. Diablo and the horse Meryl had been riding were already moseying around within the wooden fence. He came back and started on Bob.

"Soon as I get this taken care of, we gotta go out there and shoo away any buzzards to bury what's left of that calf before we have coyotes climbing the fence."

Al was going to ask who Wes meant by "we," but a sound from the back of the stables saved him the bother.

The door to the bunkroom opened, and a big man with slightly hunched shoulders came out. He nodded to Wes, ignoring Fergie and Al, then started out through the big doors. The large yellow lab that followed him, probably Ike, stayed right behind him.

"That's Bo," Wes said.

Bo hadn't spoken.

"Can he talk to people?" Fergie whispered.

"I suppose. He just prefers not to."

"Have you ever heard him talk?'

"I think he mumbled in his sleep once or twice. We just have cots back there." He nodded toward the closed door at the end of the stable.

"How can anyone get by these days without talking?"

"He manages somehow. He sure enough doesn't have a cell phone, I can tell you that. At first, I thought it was creepy. But now, I'm keen on it. I've met people in these parts who would talk to a stump. It's kind of nice not having to carry on a conversation over a plate of beans."

"Did you both work for Baron before he had to sell the spread?" Al passed the reins of Ol' Sal to Wes.

"Yep. Meryl got me the job. She knew I had fallen on some hard times. I was grateful as dammit. It was an easy switch when she came out to running the place, though she has a little firmer hand than Baron ever had."

"How about Colin?" Al asked.

"Oh, I'd run into him a few times, too, given... well, you know, how things was with him and Meryl." He winked at Al.

"Just how were things?" Fergie's eyes had narrowed again.

"Well, not to be telling tales out of school, but I guess most everyone knows he was seeing Meryl on the side, even when Ferrill was still alive."

"How does it make you feel to be working as a hand for people with whom you were once in school?" Fergie asked.

Al wouldn't have asked that, but since she had, he was anxious to see how Wes would reply.

Wes shrugged. "I've learned a lot of things in my days, 'bout as many as you two, and one thing has stuck."

"What's that?" Fergie was going to have to pry it out of him.

Wes spit on the dirt floor and started to carry Ol' Sal's saddle over to its rest. "It makes some people feel extraordinarily successful to be better off than you. Sometimes, you can turn a thing like that to your own good."

Fergie was quiet most of the way to the garage. Halfway up the stairs, on their way to freshen up, Al asked, "What do you have in mind now? This is your case, after all. I'm just tagging along."

She sighed. "I suppose we need to drive over and have a word with Baron's friends, Darren and Dewey. Their names came up."

Her words were crisp, and Al figured Fergie was still a little upset with Al's attention to Meryl. But he knew her well enough to expect that sooner or later, she would assert herself. Probably sooner. She didn't disappoint. Once they were inside the small room and he had closed the door, she turned to him.

"Take off your clothes," she said.

"What?"

She was already starting to unbutton her blouse.

"Oh, okay." He tugged off his boots and reached for his belt buckle. She was going to make him pay, and he was okay with that.

?

Fergie woke from her intense nap and felt Al's arms around her, still holding her tightly. She didn't have any problem with that, and on such a narrow bed, it was that or have one of them fall off onto the floor.

She shook off the hazy fog of what had been a pretty oddball dream. She had been back in high school, and Meryl and Ferrill had buzzed about her like two angry bees. Fergie had been the tall stalk of a flower they had felt obliged to annoy.

She'd been six foot two even in her senior year, and one of the two McCampbell twins had harped that she should be playing basketball and not want to be any part of the cheerleading squad that they were on. The school didn't have a girls' basketball team in those days, and Fergie couldn't so much as dribble a basketball, much less shoot baskets. But that didn't stop one of the twins from suggesting she join the boys' team instead of bothering them.

She hadn't even wanted to be on their stupid squad—she had merely asked about how it worked and what practice was like. What she wanted was her first date, and she had hoped it would be with Bryce Stanley, who *did* play basketball and was one of the few fellow students who could look her in the eyes.

As she lay there, feeling Al's warmth against her bare back, she couldn't for the life of her remember which twin had given her such a hard time, Meryl or Ferrill. One of them certainly had ended up with Bryce at their senior prom. She sure as hell hadn't.

She could remember in vivid detail the prom date she'd had with Al. At five eleven, he'd been shorter than her, and he had seemed to ask her reluctantly in the first place, as if he was expected to go to the dance and she was all that was left of pretty slim pickings.

He'd showed up at her house with a corsage of a cymbidium surrounded by baby's breath. She'd been wearing a dress with two strings for straps, and he'd stood in front of her, staring at those straps, then just handed her the corsage. "Here. You'd better put it on."

Neither of them were practiced and polished dancers. They had moved about like wooden figures on the dance floor. In an effort not to step on her feet, he slid his feet in his steps across the dance floor, while she bent over him like some sort of crane.

It was one of the worst and most awkward days of her life, and she was pretty sure she had heard him sigh with relief as he'd dropped her off at her front door, without so much as a kiss or handshake, and walked away.

If anyone had told her that they would be living together years later, she would have given one of the heartiest laughs she could manage. Yet, here they were.

Her eyes started to close again, and she half drifted back into that dream. Which one of the twins had it been that had given her such a hard time way back then, Meryl or Ferrill?

Though she couldn't remember which had said it, she remembered the exact words: "Why don't you go back to Africa, you overgrown giraffe."

Perhaps the words had nothing to do with her tearing the legs off a Barbie doll she hadn't cared for all that much in the first place or her ending up sprawled across her bed, her face into her pillow, sobbing like some stupid dying person.

Thinking back, she couldn't even recall what Bryce Stanley looked like. Maybe she could have checked if she hadn't tossed out her high-school yearbook long ago.

The words of whichever twin had sure stung at the time. Now, they just made her chuckle to herself as she started to fall asleep again. She guessed she had come a long way since way back then.

Chapter Seven

Baron turned the slabs of liver over in the pan, savored the sound of the sizzle, and added slices of onion across the top. He poured in half a cup of water and put the lid back over the pan.

Julie Ann, his ex, would have gotten a kick out of all this. She did like her food—she was probably about twice the size of the Goodyear blimp by now but enjoying life all the same.

He went outside the cabin to check on the ribs in the grill. When he flipped back the lid, a large puff of smoke rose in a burst to splash across his face, smelling of the mesquite he'd used along with the charcoal. They looked fine but would have to go all night.

Food made him think of Julie Ann again, with her open, smiling, girl-next-door face and her appetite for life, food, and sex. The first time he'd seen her across the dance floor of The Busted Barrel, she had looked easy to get to know. Too easy, as it turned out. After they were married, he'd physically caught her twice with other men. Who knew how many times she'd gotten away with it?

Though he had the grounds, she was the one who'd left him, even accusing him of trying to ruin her body by having Cricket. Baron had gotten full custody, a pretty unusual thing in the courtroom where that had played out.

Both Darren and Dewey, whom he'd been hanging out with at The Busted Barrel when he met Julie Ann, later admitted she had been with both of them. But as Dewey had said, "It weren't no big thing. We weren't friends with you then." Once, when they'd all had way too many beers, Darren let slip that they'd both also been with her again while she was married to Baron. If he'd been sober enough to get up out of his chair, Baron would have taken a swing at Darren. In the morning, it didn't seem to matter as much, and after she left, all that was old news.

He closed the grill lid and went back inside to check on the liver. Before he closed the door, he saw the lifting cloud of dust kicked up by a truck heading his way.

Baron was just lifting the pan off the stove when they came in, Darren first through the door and Dewey right behind him.

"That smells right good." Dewey sniffed the air. "Is there enough for all of us?"

"I suppose."

"You don't feel bad about eating your own calf?"

"Ain't none of mine now." Baron's grammar went to hell on a roller skate whenever he hung out with those two. "If she'd-a just let me keep some of the spread, we wouldn't be having to..." He stopped. "Did either of you get a glimpse of Cricket? Is she doing okay?"

"Right as rain, feisty little gal like that. She got the grit from you." Darren took the paper plate Baron held out. He carried his helping of liver over to the homemade table in the center of the cabin. A narrow bed was nestled against the far wall under the window there.

Dewey took his plate to the table. Baron slid the rest of the liver and onions onto a plate for himself. "I'm glad you fellas are keeping an eye on my former ranch. It stings like dammit not to be still runnin' it. What burns me more is Mom not giving me the money I needed for a new spread, ask how I might."

"Didn't you get some money when she bought your place?" Darren asked in spite of having a full mouth.

"Yeah, but it wasn't enough. I hadn't paid off the mortgage by a long shot."

"It's about time for the next step." Darren's plate was nearly empty. He looked over to the stove to see if there was any more liver in the pan. There wasn't.

"Just go easy and don't get greedy." Baron was still mad at his mom for having an affair with Colin while Baron's father was still alive. But she was still his mother, after all. "A hundred thousand is all I need. That should do it."

"Gotcha." Darren nodded and winked at Dewey, who winked back.

?

Al and Fergie were coming down the steps. Al was feeling rested but a little light-headed, and Fergie could barely suppress a grin.

Colin was headed their direction. "Where are you two off to?"

"We intended to go talk with Darren and Dewey, Baron's friends, to see if they have any ideas," Fergie said. "But we got a little delayed."

Al knew that if his brother, former-horn-dog Maury, were in his shoes, he would say something like, "Are you sure you mean to use the word 'little' there?" Fortunately, Al had never lived in a *Porky's* movie the way Maury had.

"Can you come to the house first? I have something important to show you." Colin turned without waiting for a response.

They followed along. It was the first time they had gone through the front door. The living room showed off a wide-open space with a fireplace on either side. Hallways at the back led to bedrooms or perhaps a den in either direction. The hallway in the middle led back to the kitchen, where Gaby was no doubt cooking away.

Everything inside the house had an austere feel to it, as if it had been furnished out of a catalog, perhaps some sort of Swedish one in which all the corners were square, giving each piece a clinical feel.

Meryl sat at one end of a brown leather couch. Cricket sat beside her with her head leaning on Meryl's shoulder. Cricket looked up at them and tried for a feeble smile. Her eyes were puffy, and she still seemed listless, compared to her earlier bustling energy.

Colin waved to the coffee table. A piece of paper lay centered on the dark polished wood. "We got a note."

"I hope you didn't handle it. There might have been fingerprints," Fergie said.

"That wouldn't have mattered. Wait until you read it." Colin plopped into a matching wing chair. "And I threw out the envelope too. It was taped to the mailbox after the regular mail had already come."

Al frowned but looked at Fergie. It was her case.

Fergie picked up the note. Al moved close to read over her shoulder. It read: "If you want Baron back, you are going to need to furnish $500,000. No law enforcement, state, local, or federal, or you get him back piece by piece."

"I don't have that kind of money," Meryl said. "Most of what I got from my first husband went toward this place. I've been carefully keeping as much back as I could, so we don't get in the scrape Baron was in, but I don't have that."

"Even if you did, we'd be talking about me being a go-between instead of finding him," Fergie said. "If we can find him first before they start setting up a drop, all this goes away."

"You can't tell much from a note like that," Colin said.

"Actually, you can," Fergie said. "There are no accidental patterns in something like this. We already know a bit about the person who dropped off the note."

"How can you—"

Fergie didn't give Colin a chance to finish. "The person who put that on your mailbox knows when your mail usually arrives, so the note could go on after the carrier had already visited but ahead of you going out to get the mail."

"And the person seems to know the exact amount of Meryl's insurance settlement," Al said.

"Those things could be explained. Someone might have done some research and observation," Colin said.

"Nevertheless, it's a starting point. We need all the traction we can get where there's not much else to go on." Fergie glanced toward Al.

"Is my daddy going to be all right?" Cricket's words quivered.

Al wished he could say something positive or encouraging. Seeing that tattoo on the man in the diner and hearing the gunfire at night on the neighboring spread had triggered stark and detailed memories of crime scenes with headless bodies, young corpses with a dozen to fifteen bullet holes each, and a kidnapping victim who'd looked like someone had tried to fillet him.

The Salvadorans were vicious, violent, and relentless. Life, even their own, meant very little to them. He hoped to hell they weren't dealing with those guys. And a sheriff who had shrugged off the heavy gunfire didn't give him anything resembling great hope for Baron or themselves. And they had to think about the possibility of some sort of inside job, since someone knew a lot about Meryl and Colin's lives. But that could have been learned from observation and a little digging and was offset by the hint of brutal violence. It was all pretty much a muddle.

Al and Fergie looked at each other. Neither of them had anything they could say or guarantee to the little girl.

Chapter Eight

Fergie stepped outside the front door and let Al close it behind them. She took a deep breath and took in the scent of dust, the horses, and the cattle.

"That overwhelming whiff of cow pie you're getting pretty well sums up what we have to go on here," Al said.

"They're not cows. They're steers," she said.

"I knew that. Steer pies, then. But there are aspects of this case that sure smell funny."

"Give me a minute here." Fergie saw Meryl walking off by herself. Meryl's hand went up to her face a couple of times, and Fergie felt an itch to know if her former classmate was crying.

Meryl's walk out into the green-and-brown pasture seemed aimless, yet she managed to miss every steer pie. Her shoulders shook.

"Are you okay?" Fergie asked as she came up closer.

"Yeah, fine. Just swell." Meryl turned. Her eyes were red. She brushed at them with the back of one hand. She had to look up, since Fergie was a head taller.

The day was heating up, and the sun was climbing high, where it could roll up its sleeves and really let them have it.

As Meryl faced Fergie, she was struck once more by how youthful Meryl looked. A jealous wave of envy swept through her, even though she was trying to be objective. But dammit, the woman just radiated youthfulness, enough to turn Fergie's stomach... and to make her want to drag Al upstairs to their bedroom again.

Al and Fergie had been to a get-together for some former class-mates not too long back—not a full-blown reunion but a cozy enough cluster to present a reasonable sample. She had been struck by the harsh reality of the years, how gravity and wear had had its way with some of them, while others hadn't even made it so far. Some of those in the group had praised Fergie for staying so lean and fit, which contributed in part to her looking years younger. She'd heard one of the male spouses whisper to another of the other women in the group, "Why did some people bring their mothers?"

Yet Meryl looked and acted years younger even than Fergie. She felt that twinge again. Maybe it was genetics with the twins. Meryl's skin looked smooth and taut, with barely a hint of wrinkles. Even with how red they were at the moment, she had a sparkle and luster to her eyes. Maybe she did a boot-camp fitness regime and could afford what it took to look the way she did. Fergie shook herself and snapped out of it. "What is it?" she asked. "What's bothering you most?"

"Oh, poor little Cricket. She's going through so much. It breaks my heart."

"She can seem pretty chipper at times too." Fergie didn't know whether to reach out a comforting hand or not.

"Kids can seem resilient, but they pick up things that can scar them for life."

"Did that happen to you?"

Meryl looked off to where a group of steers was ambling closer, acting like they were nibbling at grass but probably drawn by the sight and sound of humans.

"We didn't really hang out all that much in high school, did we?" Meryl blinked and rubbed at her eyes again, which was only making them redder.

"There was a lot of cow-flop class distinction back then."

"Well, Ferrill and I weren't in the absolute top layer. Maybe the second tier or somewhere thereabouts."

"And I wasn't anywhere near that rarified strata."

"All that means so little, eventually," Meryl said. "Life evens us up and levels us off."

"But you have all this." Fergie waved a hand at the spread around them.

"I'd trade it all to have my son back."

Fergie sensed Meryl was as emotionally vulnerable as she could get, so she picked her words with care. "What do you know about these friends of Baron, Darren and Dewey?"

"It's Darren Stem and Dewey Lewis. They were thick as fleas with Baron. Darren inherited the spread from his father, who climbed into a bottle and drowned. The father was a failed cattleman. I don't know how the son is getting by. He did come into some pretty hefty cash when some outfit paid him to put up one of those communication towers on a corner of his land he wasn't using anyway."

Fergie hesitated to explore the next possibility. "Is there any reason Baron would just take off and leave his daughter behind?"

"I can't think of one."

"Did he view losing the ranch and you having to bail him out as a failure?"

"It *was* a failure." The bravest of the approaching steers got close enough to sniff at Meryl. She shooed it away.

"I hear he claimed the marijuana patch wasn't his."

"It was on his land. He should have, at the very least, known about it. He's lucky it was burned before the law arrived, though it broke Baron when he lost his hay crop and some of his cattle. You need to have some money back if you're going to run a spread, with all the ups and downs that go with that."

"So you bought the spread with your money, right?"

"Yeah. Colin and I keep our money separate. I never had all that much, until recently. He sold his mechanical-engineering firm that made all kinds of products for oil rigs a year or so before we married. We both agreed to one tough prenup agreement."

"Did he get a lot for his company?"

"Seven million, yet he was still living in a condo."

"Colin could pay any ransom demand, couldn't he?"

"He could." Meryl looked away. Her shoulders shook again. Her words trembled when she spoke. "But we'll have to wait and see. We have a lot going on together, but money is one of those walls between us."

"Look, I've got to get going," Fergie said. "Since you've received a note beginning a ransom process, you're looking at a heightened urgency here. I still think you ought to call the FBI or the sheriff, unless you don't trust her."

Meryl turned away, her shoulders shaking harder. She waved a hand. Fergie didn't know whether that meant good-bye or her being shooed away.

Chapter Nine

"I'm starting to wonder if Colin didn't ask this favor of me just because it would be cheaper." Fergie held the steering wheel tightly and gave Al a quick glance. "He could have afforded a top-shelf detective agency."

"You're top shelf in my book," Al said.

"I wasn't fishing for a compliment. What if he wanted someone a little incompetent who would act like they're doing something but would just be thrashing around?"

"Do you feel like you're thrashing around?"

"Of course I do. These are early days, and there's very little to go on."

"You've worked kidnapping cases before."

"Yeah. Sure. But when I could, I passed them on to the FBI or once to the Texas Rangers. I did work a few cases myself, when that seemed the best way to go."

"Then you know such cases start slow, and then the layers begin to peel away."

"And as often as not, the kidnapped victim is found dead or never found."

"I'm not sure about adults, but only one in ten thousand abductions of children end in death," Al said, "although I don't think that stat allows for kids who end up in the human trafficking biz, and that figure is higher with anything related to gang activity."

As if he had said the magic words, a motorcycle came over the rise in the oncoming lane.

Al gave it a scant glance. Far more fine, upstanding folk rode motorcycles than gang bangers. Then, too, a lone biker was hardly a gang.

"He's turning around," Fergie said.

She was right. The motorcycle slowed, made a U-turn, and was accelerating toward them. No one was on the road going that direction. Al looked the other way—no one there, either.

The bike came up on them fast, pulled right up beside Fergie's window, and waved for them to pull over.

Fergie shook her head.

"Is that the same goofy son of a bitch from the diner?" Al could see the forearm with the tattoo proudly displayed.

"Looks like it to me, although I have my hands full with driving."

The biker got ahead of them and hit his brakes enough to slow them. When it looked like he was going to come to a stop, Fergie swerved out into the other empty lane and shot around him. The biker sped up until he was right on their tail. Then he pulled up close to Fergie's window and gave the gang hand sign, the devil's horns.

"We're almost to Darren and Dewey's place, and this doesn't look like it's going to let up." Al opened the glove box and got his Sig Sauer out of its sock. He slipped it inside his belt at the small of his back.

"What are you going to do?"

"Whatever's necessary," he said.

Fergie eased the car onto the shoulder, and the biker pulled in behind them. Al hopped out the passenger door and headed toward the biker while he was still getting his bike onto its kickstand.

The guy swung to stare hard-eyed at Al. "You two da ones from the diner, no?"

"We were there, yes."

"I am Gino." He struggled with his English a little, but he had enough of it to threaten. "I want you to know so you can die now."

Gino pulled a long knife out of a sheath inside his right motorcycle boot.

"What makes you do that?" Al asked.

Gino grinned, a wicked, evil sneer. "I have a sickness."

"You should take a pill for it." Al took the pistol out from behind his back and held it down at his side. "A lead one."

The Salvadoran looked at the gun then down at his knife. He spit into the grass beside the shoulder, slid the knife back into its sheath, hopped onto his motorcycle, angrily kick-started it, and took off. He turned to head back the way he'd been going. He didn't look back.

As Al slid back into his seat and put the pistol away, Fergie said, "Gosh, I hope I'm wrong about what I'm thinking."

"I hope you are, too, but suspect you aren't. All that shooting I heard in the night and now this. If there's a whole mess of Salvadorans nested up between Meryl and Colin's place and that of Darren and Dewey, we have one real tangle to unravel here."

"If it's these MS-13 dudes behind Baron being missing," Fergie said, "I don't look forward to doing whatever is going to need doing."

Al kept an eye on the road behind them and thought he saw the biker pull over, perhaps to watch them from as far away as he could get.

The gateway to Darren and Dewey's spread was marked by a weathered frame of four-by-four boards that was beginning to take a slight lean to the right but without the touristy charm of the tower in Pisa.

The lane was a two-rut dirt invitation to turn into a mud bowl at the first rain. When dry, a brown cloud could rise each time a vehicle passed between the open fields that were tangles of weeds, cacti, scrub bushes, and piles of rocks here and there. A dust cloud lifted and followed them.

The land in that part of Texas was flatter than the hill country back where Al lived. Still, there were swells to the fields and former pastures around them, swells like in a sea when it's starting to get a surly mood on. He couldn't see forever in each direction, but he could see an occasional old live oak tree, and they told him something.

When a pasture is active, with cattle feeding, they will eat at the lower limbs of tree, a habit called goating a tree. The trees Al could see didn't have the typical flat bottoms from that. These trees had once been that way, but their lower limbs were growing back and hanging down. No one had let cattle pasture there for some time—no sheep, goats, or even emus, either. All livestock took some work, and the place looked like it hadn't seen a lick of work in quite a spell.

As they rounded a hillock covered in buffalo grass, Al could see a ramshackle farmhouse ahead. A pickup the reddish brown of primer was just pulling up by the porch, a pale brown cloud of dust settling behind it. Al couldn't tell whether the truck had just come in from the way he and Fergie were or if it had been elsewhere on the ranch, if indeed it was a ranch.

Next to the pale, weathered boards of the farmhouse, a pile of fallen planks and timbers marked what might once have been a bunkhouse that rested in a clutter of a heap.

As they pulled up, two guys were getting out of the truck.

Al rolled down his window as Fergie took her car within a few feet.

One fellow looked like he was going to reach inside the truck then decided differently. "What do you folks want?"

"Are you Darren and Dewey?"

"We used to be." The tall, dirty-blond one with a ponytail chuckled.

"What?" Fergie glanced back and forth between them.

"I'm just funning you. I'm Darren. This lovely specimen of manhood is Dewey." He waved a hand toward the pudgy guy in bib overalls with a dark buzz cut.

"I wonder if we could talk to you about Baron. Seems he's gone missing, and we've been asked to look for him."

"Who are you, the law?"

"We used to be."

"Well, I was once an infant, but I'm over that." Darren looked to Dewey, who chuckled.

Al tried to look around the yard area, but there was little to see from where they were. In no direction could he see anything that looked like a productive ranch or even farm—no hay fields, cotton, or oil wells. The house had been a pale blue once but had been reduced by the wind to a mottled grey where it wasn't showing silvery wood. A windmill against one end of the building had bent at the middle to topple to one side. The metal livestock-watering tub at its base looked empty. He couldn't see or smell any cattle. A tractor that looked like it was from the 1920s showed bare metal covered in orange rust. Along the far edge of a weed-stubbled field, a row of cottonwoods grew in a line, marking where there was or had been a creek. The whole place had a desolate look about it.

"Are you friends with Baron Fieldings?" Fergie asked.

"Yeah," Darren said. He and Dewey looked at each other.

"When did you last see him?"

"A week or so back, maybe longer than that." They looked at each other again.

"Do you know anything that might help us find him?"

"Nope." Dewey spoke for the first time, and his voice sounded rusty and little used.

"Don't you want to help us find your friend?" Fergie asked.

Darren leaned low so he could see in through Al's window to look toward Fergie.

"I'll tell you what I told the sheriff's people. We don't know where he is. We'd like to hear from him. We surely would."

Dewey nodded along.

"We'll let his kin know if we know anything about him, or maybe the sheriff," Darren said. "Now you folks ought to mosey along, 'cause this property is posted, and we didn't ask you onto it." He and Dewey stepped back, ending any opportunity for discussion.

Fergie fired up the engine and turned her car to head back out the lane. "Did you think Darren and Dewey were being pretty disingenuous?"

"They're on edge about something," Al said. "What I wanted to ask them was how they could afford a ranch if they're not raising any crop that I could see."

"We never even got out of the car," Fergie said. "That was the first drive-through interview I've ever conducted."

"Do you think we should have done something else?"

"I don't know how we could have."

Fergie waited until they were almost to the gate before she spoke again. "I think I'd like to know what makes these Muppet mutts tick. Are they brothers, lovers, or just two pals who smoked a lot of the same stuff?"

Al shrugged. "If these are Baron's two best friends, I now give us less hope of ever finding him."

"Yeah. Their enthusiasm was pretty underwhelming."

?

The white stone ranchero home had a flagstone patio in its courtyard. Mauricio, the leader and shot-caller of the *clica*, came out of the house and saw Isaác sharpening a pile of machetes.

"Why you doin' tha'?"

"*Porque...*"

"*En inglés.*" Mauricio was trying to get them all to speak in English as much as possible. Orders from higher up were to fit in better as part of the training and also to discourage tattoos. His own body was covered with tats, with MS-13 right across his forehead. His cheeks and neck were also covered in old ink, as well as his arms and legs. His late father had had as many tattoos when he had been a paramilitary in the *Farabundo Marti para la Liberación Nacional,* fighting as a guerilla in the insurgency against the Salvadoran government.

Where the tats had once spread fear, they now made the Maras too easy to identify. Whether it was the feds or other gangs, they were at constant war and needed to be less visible. The young ones, the recruits, the *chequeos,* they didn't understand. They wanted to command fear. They wanted people to shake and tremble when they entered a room. That had been the way, the old way. The Maras were trying to be more subtle, to fit in and not give themselves away. Some of them understood. Others, like that fire ant, Gino, had a thicker head about it.

"I'm honing these," Isaác said. "Remember how the heads used to pop off when these were sharp. No?"

José, sitting at a patio table on the other side of the patio, grinned, although he had yet to sever his first head. He was still a *chequeo*, like Gino. At seventeen and just under 120 pounds, he had barely survived his initiation beatdown. A couple of initiates had not fared as well. Glad to be alive and serving, he had been busy cleaning and loading weapons—M-16s, AK-47s, and a couple of MAC-10s.

"I hear from the others out working on the landing field that those rancheros on the next place, they run a meth lab." José rubbed at his sweaty brow with a blue bandana. He nodded in the direction of Darren and Dewey's place.

A load of M-16s all the way from Honduras was due to arrive that night. He'd also been promised some very special ordnance as well, something with some real kick and firepower. Mauricio had wanted the landing strip as ready as possible.

"Is tha' right?" Isaác jerked his head toward Mauricio. "A good way to make some dollars other than jacking trucks. Wha' you say?"

"If it's true." Mauricio nodded.

A motorcycle, its engine revving in excitement, came tearing up the lane toward them. That half-crazy fool Gino was behind the handlebars. He waved with one arm as he approached.

"Hey. You never guess what."

"What?"

"I saw that dude and his giant redhead chick from the diner."

"And?"

"He pulled a gun on me, man." Gino went over and picked up one of the MAC-10s. "We gonna see how that goes next time 'round."

"You didn't ask for permission to engage anyone," Mauricio said. The lower-ranking Maras always needed their leader's permission to act. "We'll talk about that later. You sure it was them?"

"Sí. Yes. The same ones."

Mauricio and Isaác had been in the bathroom when the state troopers arrived. They had barely explained their way out of Gino being arrested and had to leave without eating.

"You just see them going past?"

"Kind of. I hung back after I see them. They looked like they went into the next place up the road."

"Hmm." Mauricio would have liked to know more about that spread, especially if there was a rich meth lab to knock off and piles of cash besides. "They didn't see you?"

"No. They think they scare me away with a gun. But I hang back, follow them."

"They're armed?"

"The man was, sure 'nough."

"In that case." Mauricio went to the table and picked up an M-16. "Okay. Let's say we ride." He headed for one of the trucks in the drive. Isaác took one of the machetes and a MAC-10. He headed for another truck.

"Wha' 'bout me?" José shouted.

"You ride with Isaác."

Gino turned his motorcycle around and led the way.

?

Fergie turned out onto the two-lane road leading back toward Meryl and Colin's place. Al was looking out his side window, thinking over what little he could tell them about their digging so far. For being so-called best friends of Baron, those two back there had been far from cooperative.

"Ahem. Take a peek," Fergie said.

A short caravan of two trucks led by a motorcycle was coming their way in the other lane.

"Oh dear." Al flipped open the glove box and got out both guns. He jacked a shell into the chamber and slipped the Glock to Fergie. He rolled down his window. "The first round is a scare round. Then we aim for their machines."

Fergie rolled down her window and clenched the steering wheel tighter. "Yep. It's that same squirrelly little dude, and he has friends," she said. "Those look like the trucks that were parked outside the diner."

The thing about that sort of surprise engagement was not to hesitate. He didn't have to tell Fergie that. She floored the gas and headed right at the group of them.

Al could see the eyes of Gino, the motorcyclist, growing wider. He was first in line and would have little chance of surviving.

A hundred feet from them, the motorcycle veered hard right, bouncing onto the shoulder and kicking up a spray of gravel as it dipped down into a shallow ditch then slammed into a three-strand barbed wire fence just after the rider jumped to one side.

The truck following the bike veered hard to its left, aiming to get into the lane Fergie had vacated. It was close enough to see a driver's face covered with dark ink.

Al aimed for its radiator, squeezing off three rounds right where it should be, and he was rewarded with steam hissing out in a spray as the truck went into the ditch on the far side of the road.

Holding the steering wheel tightly with her right hand, Fergie fired a row of shots that ran across the top of the windshield of the next truck, dropping the safety glass in a shower of sparkling diamonds onto the laps and into the faces of the driver and passenger. The truck was already heading right to get off the road and smashed into the motorcycle, just missing the guy on the ground, who was scrambling on hands and knees to get out of the way.

Al looked back at both trucks off the road, one in a cloud of steam, and a motorcycle that he hoped was going to need about a year in the shop. None of the machines were in any kind of shape to turn and come in pursuit. "I'd say that went well."

"As well as it could." She handed her gun to Al. It was warm to the touch.

He reloaded both guns from the box of ammo and put them back into the glove box.

Fergie was humming to herself as they went down the road, finally turning into the lane where Meryl and Colin lived.

Chapter Ten

As soon as Fergie pulled her car up to the front of the ranch house, Meryl came running toward them.

Colin opened the front door then stood there, one arm up and resting against the door frame, and watched her run.

She got to their car just as Al and Fergie were climbing out. She came to a stop, panting, and gasped, "There was a call. Colin said the voice was muffled, disguised. They asked for five hundred thousand dollars. Can you believe it? Five hundred thousand dollars!" Each word climbed in pitch and volume.

Before either of them could say anything, Meryl got her wind and said, "And do you know what Colin said? He said no. *No.* Can you believe it? Then he said he wanted proof Baron was alive."

"Oh, he probably shouldn't have said that." Fergie closed her car door.

Al figured Colin might have been thinking of something like a photo with Baron holding up a dated newspaper. Depending on who they were dealing with, providing proof could get far worse. He didn't mention the time J. Paul Getty III's ear got cut off by Calabrian bandits, who sent it to the parents when they were slow to cough up the requested ransom.

A car was coming up the lane. As it neared, Al could make out the markings of the county sheriff's department. When it pulled up behind Fergie's car, the sheriff herself climbed out of the passenger seat. Her deputy Took got out of the driver's side and just stood there, towering over the cruiser. He squinted at each of them in turn.

Rosa hitched up her gun belt and walked over to Meryl.

Colin closed the door to the house and came toward them. "I told you they said not to call her."

"You're lucky she did," Rosa said. "I need to stay on top of this. No note or anything?"

"Just an idiot demand for half a million," Colin said.

"He told them he wanted proof Baron is alive," Meryl said.

"Oh, you probably shouldn't have said that." The sheriff shook her head.

"Any chance any of this involves the Maras we passed on the road coming this way?" Fergie asked.

"Passed?"

"If you'd come that way, you probably would've seen them getting their trucks and a wrecked bike towed back to where they came from."

Rosa looked over at Fergie's car and turned back to her. "You say you had a face-to-face confrontation with these so-called gang members, and you didn't get a scratch. Your car has no bullet holes, but your story does."

Fergie shrugged.

Al was glad Fergie didn't press it—far easier to shrug it off than explain opening fire out on the roads of the sheriff's county.

"Are they going to call again?" Rosa asked Colin.

"I guess they have to if they want to set up a drop-off of the cash or anything."

"Are you going to pay the ransom?"

"No way," Colin said. "That's why I brought in these two hotshots—to find Baron before it comes to that."

"Well, good luck with that. Humpf." The sheriff rolled her eyes.

"Will you tap our phone or something?" Colin asked.

"I'll keep doing what I've been doing, which is everything I can, despite any vote of no confidence. Now, does anyone else have anything to say?" She looked at Fergie and then at Al. "I didn't think so."

The sheriff lumbered back to the cruiser and climbed in. Soon, it was rolling back out the drive, kicking up a cloud of brown dust.

Fergie shook her head as she watched the car. "She's on the take."

"Could be," Al said. "But I doubt it will do any good to ask her."

"We just have to work harder and faster, maybe do something drastic." Fergie watched the cloud of dust settle as the cruiser rolled out of sight.

"What do you have in mind?"

Fergie nodded toward the stairs up to their room. Meryl and Colin were both looking at them.

Al started to follow her.

"What are you guys going to do?" Colin asked.

"I guess I'll find out in a couple of minutes," Al said.

Halfway up the stairs, Colin called, "What should I expect?"

"We never discussed what you planned to pay me." Fergie kept moving up the stairs.

"I thought you would do it as a favor, a personal favor."

"Yet you have money." Fergie paused with her hand on the wooden railing.

"It's why I do."

Fergie shook her head and turned to continue up the stairs.

"You're really not going to let me know what you have in mind?"

"I don't think so," she said.

"Well, just remember who's not paying you."

Colin turned and walked away. Al said in a low voice, "The most dangerous person you can come across is one who thinks he is intelligent but has slightly missed that mark and has replaced it with arrogance and the socially awkward habit of saying the candid-but-wrong thing."

"You're singing to the choir, Al." Fergie went inside the tiny room, which had grown dank but was too hot and dusty to be called "clammy." When Al closed the door, she said, "I also never met anyone who I am more sure still has his original dime."

"I thought you dated him once."

"I'm just recalling that it was his wanting to go Dutch on dates that had something to do with why that ended." She tilted her head at him. "You're thinking something. I can practically hear the wheels turning. What is it?"

"I'm just musing about the parts of this that seem to have a simple answer. Yet I suspect there are hidden complexities."

"Aren't there always?"

"Yeah, but I don't want either of us to get hurt because of that."

?

Baron had stretched out in a hammock in the shadowy side of the cabin. A small breeze, dry and dusty, swept through, but it was enough to help him doze off. It seemed he had been asleep only seconds when he felt a cloth handkerchief press against his nose and mouth. His eyes battled to flutter open, and he struggled to rise, resisting the sweet chemical smell.

When he did awaken, his eyes snapped open. He was in the cabin by himself. He tried to stand from the straight-backed chair, but something held him in place. Silver duct tape went around each wrist. He couldn't see his ankles but couldn't move them. He suspected they were bound by tape, too, each ankle to the bottom of a chair leg. He began to yell.

After a good ten minutes, the door to the cabin opened, and Darren and Dewey came in. Darren shook his head and said softly, "Now. Now."

Dewey was chuckling. "It's kinda like space. No one can hear you scream."

"What's wrong with you guys? This isn't funny. Cut me loose."

"You see, there's a problem with that, Baron," Darren said. "We need your cooperation to make this work."

"I'm cooperating."

"I doubt if you'd be all the way willing if you knew just what it's going to take."

"Hey, those calf ribs ought to be just about done by now." Baron couldn't do anything about the quiver in his voice. He had just noticed that Dewey was holding bolt cutters low at his side in one hand.

"Oh, we'll be eating those ribs. You can count on that," Darren said. "You're right-handed, aren't you?"

"Y-Yes."

"Then the left little finger, Dewey." Darren held up a hand. "Maybe a little tape first." He tore off a six-inch length of duct tape and stepped closer to place it across Baron's mouth, though Baron tossed his head from side to side, resisting.

Dewey lifted the bolt cutters until he held them in both hands. He started walking slowly toward Baron.

Baron tried as hard as he could to scream. But all he could do was make desperate bubbling, gulping sounds behind the tape as Dewey came closer.

?

Gino rode in the second tow truck. His bike rested in the bed of the truck being towed. "No one does this to Gino," he muttered.

"Who's Gino?" the driver asked.

"I am Gino, and I am one very angry Gino just at this moment."

"That was your bike?"

"Still is."

"I think we'll be able to get it running for you, but it ain't gonna be pretty. We'll need more time for body work."

"Just so it runs," Gino said.

"Yeah. The trucks'll be easy. Looks like pop in a radiator on one, a windshield for the other. I got guys going through a scrap yard right now. We'll check everything else and get you all back on the road."

The truck driver's name was Andy, if the sign on the truck meant anything, but Gino didn't think it did. He was a guy Mauricio had met in prison. Andy ran a chop shop in a metal-sided warehouse on the outside edge of Houston, where they had brought stolen cars in the past. But his guys could fix vehicles as well as strip them in minutes.

"Just so we going again soon."

"Oh, you'll be going again. Don't you worry about that." The driver rubbed a greasy finger under his nose. "Like I said, you won't be pretty. But you'll go."

"Screw pretty. There's a place where I'm gonna need to fix some people. I just need to get there."

The driver shut up the rest of the way to his shop, probably glad he wasn't one of the people Gino wanted to fix.

Chapter Eleven

Wes was mucking out one of the horse stalls when Al and Fergie went into the stables.

"Do you mind helping us saddle the two horses we had before?" Fergie asked.

"Ol' Sal and Bob? Sure thing. I don't mind a bit. It's what I do around here."

He smiled, and Al wished he hadn't. The front hole in his teeth loomed as large and dark as the opening to Carlsbad Caverns. It wouldn't have surprised Al if a bat flew out of that gaping space.

Wes leaned his pitchfork against the stall's wall and went right to work saddling the horses. He brought the mare in from the corral first and had her ready to go in minutes.

"Do you ever think about those days we shared when we were all back in school together?" Al took the reins of Ol' Sal when Wes handed them to him.

"As little as possible." Wes bent over his task and didn't look up at him.

"Why?"

"I don't think we were ever the cool students, were we?"

"But you have your whole life since then."

Wes shook his head. "I try most days to be like Bo Melford. He don't hardly speak. He don't watch TV or read or take nature walks. He just does his chores, eats, and climbs into his cot with that dog at his feet."

"That doesn't sound like much of a life." Al stroked the side of Ol' Sal's neck. Wes was almost done saddling Bob. "Please tell me you're a bit more active than that."

"Well, truth be told, I drink a bit."

Fergie frowned. "Maybe you can tell me this. What is Baron like?"

"What do you mean?"

"Is he bubbly, sullen, cheerful, or what?"

"I suppose all of those, at one time or another."

"Do you know of anywhere he might have gone on his own? Does he have a special place? Maybe a park, a motel, or any place he might stay with a lady friend?"

"No."

Wes ambled off as soon as he was done.

He was out of sight, but Fergie stood next to Bob and leaned her face to rest her forehead on Bob's neck.

"What are you doing?"

"Just taking a second or two to appreciate my life, every aspect of it. Even this, coming out to thrash around mostly unsuccessfully at rounding up a single missing person. I just have a whole lot more reason to feel alive than some people."

"I wouldn't judge Wes too harshly. He's probably back in the other room busting open a piñata even as we speak."

"Thanks for that."

"For what?"

"The attempt at cheering me up, feeble as it was." She swung herself up into the saddle, and they took off.

The thermometer had been on seventy degrees when they set out, but the sun was climbing and making itself felt. They'd both worn their fishing caps, ball caps with the single bill out front, so their ears were going to take a licking.

The hay fields on one side and grazing clumps of cattle around them provided little variety. The horses wisely steered clear of a patch of loose rock and prickly-pear cactus that almost certainly held a rat-tlesnake or two.

The ride would have been as relaxing as being on his fishing boat on the water, with lots to look about and see, and a nice breeze sweeping over them. But their reason for going out to the extreme edges of the ranch intruded.

Al wondered, as they bounced gently up and down in their saddles, what the sheriff was doing about Baron. Was she questioning Darren and Dewey and getting more than Al and Fergie had? Had she looked around on the ranch next to Meryl's? Did she have deputies looking around in all the logical places where Baron might be held?

They came to the far end of Meryl's spread, where a sturdy cattle fence separated it from the adjacent ranch. Al could hear distant pops and occasional shouting.

"What's going on over there?" Fergie stood in her stirrups to see farther.

"I have no idea. If I had to guess, I'd say it sounds more like the boot camp I went through years ago rather than anything else. It sure as hell doesn't sound like ranching."

They sat on their horses and looked out across land that rose in a slow swell before it finally blocked their view.

Al was still muddling things through his head. Some things seemed possible, though far from obvious yet. Other things seemed less possible but for that reason equally probable. And the people? They seemed a jolly mix—it was hard to tell about them. Except Cricket. If ever he'd had a daughter, he would have welcomed one like her.

As if on cue, he heard hooves thudding against the dirt and turned in his saddle to see Cricket riding Diablo at a brisk pace toward them. Al wished he had her eleven-year-old confidence in riding a stallion like that. But he suspected that if he tried to mount Diablo, he'd get thrown seven ways from Sunday.

She reined in beside them. Her red cowgirl boots and jeans were worn enough to indicate that she probably rode as often as she could. She matched them with a white blouse with pearl buttons and a white cowgirl hat. The hat showed she was smarter than Fergie and Al—her ears wouldn't be pink at the end of the day. "What are you two doing?"

"Everything we can to get your dad back to you," Al said.

"Oh. It looked like you were sitting and thinking."

"Sometimes, that's the right thing to do for a spell first, so you don't wind up stepping in something," Fergie said.

That made Cricket giggle, but the smile slid off her face. More pops sounded in the distance.

"How long have new folks been on this ranch?" Al nodded toward the sounds.

"Less than a year. The place sat idle for a spell."

"Let me ask you something," Fergie said. "Is there a way around the next ranch?"

"Yep. If you're on a horse or on foot, there's an open stretch of gravel and sand that runs along under that mesa yonder. But you don't want to be there when it rains. It's a wash."

"Have you ever been there?"

"Sure. There's a gate back yonder at the far end of our place. Well, Auntie Gran's spread now." Cricket lowered her head but was soon patting Diablo and straightening his mane. "You can get up on top of the mesa and look around. I've done that before. Sometimes, there isn't much to do out here, and I get bored. I had lots of friends when we lived in town. But here..." She waved a hand at the ranch around her.

"You have Diablo here, though," Fergie said.

"Yeah, and he's the best thing, except for my dad. I surely hope you find him."

"We do too." Fergie gave the adjacent ranch another look. "We're going to do everything we can to get him to you, where he belongs.

Now, what say you show us the way back to the ranch house. But don't go too fast. We don't want to see Al here fall and break his crown."

Cricket chuckled, spun her horse, and took off at a trot but then slowed to wait for them.

Al was thinking maybe a more subtle invasive visit was in order. He didn't want to discuss that with Fergie until they were alone.

Soon enough, they were riding up to the stable.

Cricket busied herself putting her own horse away. Al and Fergie handed their reins over to Wes.

While he was taking the saddles off their horses, Wes said, "I was in town, getting some personal supplies..."

"Something liquid?" Fergie asked.

"You want me to tell this?"

"Go ahead."

"And some guy comes up to me and pulls me aside. He wanted to know what you two were up to."

"What did you say?"

"That I didn't have a clue."

"What was he like?" Al handed over the reins to Ol' Sal, since Wes was done with Bob and had given him a gentle slap on the rump to move him toward the corral.

"Kinda spooky sort of Latino dude. He had a low, hard body, like he was made out of solid muscle, and he had the hardest eyes I've ever seen."

"You didn't get his name?"

"Hell no. Someone looking like that? You don't think I want to get to know everyone who follows me into a liquor store."

"What did you get?"

"Whatever was on sale. You know. Some Texas-made vodka was half off. Being a hand on a ranch is a regular plate of beans and not too much else. But hell, I'm glad to have the work." He tossed Ol' Sal's saddle onto its rest and gave her a pat on the rump that sent her clomping out into the corral.

?

They were going up the stairs to their room when Colin's white Land Cruiser came tearing up the lane to the house in a boil of dust. He slammed on the brakes and came to a nearly sliding stop. He swung the driver's-side door open and popped out to yell up at them. "You'll not believe what was in the mailbox this time."

He held up a yellow bubble wrap mailer, torn open at one end.

"What is it?" Fergie started back down the stairs.

"Take a look. Just take a look."

Fergie peeked inside. "Al?"

Al stepped closer. Inside, in a clear plastic sandwich bag, was a finger. "I hope you didn't touch the plastic bag. There might still be prints on it."

"Hell no. I only had to see the damned thing."

"Any way of knowing if it's Baron's?" Fergie asked.

"By looking at it? No. Of course not." Colin's voice had taken on a higher pitch and an exasperated edge, a sound that carried.

Meryl came running toward them from the ranch house. Her eyes were wide even as she ran.

Al took as close a look as he dared without touching anything. From the finger's nail, he could see it was the left little finger of an adult male. The end where it had been severed from the hand was more pinched and smashed than cut. He'd seen wounds on a man's hands after he had held them up, trying futilely to fend off a swinging machete. Where those fingers had been severed, the cuts were clean, and the wounds had bled more. Whatever had severed the finger he was looking at had squashed some of the veins closed, so there'd been less bleeding. That the finger *had* bled at all told Al it had come off a living person.

Meryl reached them, panting hard. She moved to stand close enough to Colin to take a quick look into the bag then spun away, bent at the waist, and looked ready to throw up. But wracking dry heaves were all she could manage.

When she finally got a grip on herself, she straightened, shaky and with watering eyes. "That's just too much. Too, too much. First they want five hundred thousand. Now this."

"What do you think?" Colin asked Fergie.

"I think that at the least you ought to call the sheriff and maybe consider the FBI."

"You think you two aren't up to handling this?" Colin stared at them. Meryl pressed close to his side with her mouth open, but she seemed incapable of speech.

"I guess we'll see," Fergie said.

"No one can do anything!" Meryl pushed away from Colin. She spun and started running toward the house. "No one can do a damned thing!"

?

Gino bent over the motorcycle. He put more rubbing compound on the rag he held and began to rub the fender and the side of the gas tank. What rubbing compound did, he knew, was to take tiny scratches and sort of melt the paint around them until they appeared smooth again. He shook his head. That wasn't going to be enough where rows of scratches and scrapes made the bike look like a tiger had clawed at it. The bike needed to go to a body shop for a complete makeover before he would be proud to be seen riding it again.

Steps sounded behind him. He looked up at Mauricio.

"You better give it a rest for now. You know what we gotta prepare for."

Gino nodded but kept rubbing. He wasn't making much progress at getting all the scratches out, anyway. He had fired up the bike, and it ran well enough. But he had bought it new, and the way it looked hurt his heart and made him as full of angry, burning rage as he'd ever been.

"The trucks run again as well. Now, you'd better get some rest like the others. For tonight."

Gino hung the rag over the gas tank and stood up straight. Okay, he would go lie down, but he doubted he would sleep. Someone was going to pay for his bike's sad look—pay early, pay often, and pay hard.

Chapter Twelve

Al and Fergie climbed the stairs to their deluxe cracker-box accommodations long enough to wash their faces, clean up a bit, and load a small backpack each with binoculars, a compass, their pistols, and ammo. They each filled a canteen with tap water and were good to go. Just the sort of thing for the picnic they had in mind. By the time they entered the kitchen, Colin and Cricket were already seated at the table and had started their lunch. Three empty places had been set at the table.

"Sorry, Gaby. We're going to take off for a short spell." Fergie looked longingly at the chicken enchiladas with mole sauce, a guacamole salad, and a bowl of pico de gallo.

"I fix you somethin' to go." Gaby went to the oven and took out some tortillas that were warming.

"Where are you off to?" Colin asked.

"Where's Meryl?" Fergie asked.

Once she had handed Al and Fergie each a delicious-smelling small paper bag, Gaby scurried around the seated two, pouring more iced tea and bringing a basket warmer containing more tortillas for them.

"She's a little under the weather." Colin gave a tiny nod in Cricket's direction.

The sheriff had sent out a deputy to collect the finger. No one had told Cricket about that. When Rosa had called Meryl to follow up, the sheriff was able to confirm that the finger had belonged to Baron. Her final say was that they were to let her handle it.

"I wonder what the hands in the stable are having," Fergie said.

Colin came close to chuckling, but his mood was too dark. "They're getting the same thing we are. I hope ol' Wes didn't spring that story about nothing but a plate of beans on you two as well. I never met a man who felt more sorry for himself. He should be more like Bo, though truth be told, it's hard to tell what Bo feels or thinks about. He's only got half as much personality as Ike."

"I like Bo. He always gives Diablo extra oats." Cricket looked around at each of them, daring them to say something bad about Bo.

Al and Fergie eased their way out of the kitchen with a thanks to Gaby. They headed across the dirt yard to the secondary buildings.

"My butt's still a little sore. Are you sure about this?" Al asked.

"Has to be done." But Fergie didn't look any happier than Al felt about another session in the saddles.

Once inside the stable, Al and Fergie brought in Ol' Sal from the corral first. She seemed the easiest to handle. Al was trying to remember the steps of how to saddle her properly and had just taken down her blanket when Wes came out into the stable from the small bunkhouse end.

"Oh, my auntie's fanny. You'll be riding her backwards if you aren't careful. Here, let me give you a hand."

Wes's movements were quick and sure compared to the fumbling Al had been doing. His efficiency at dealing with horses' tack renewed Al's appreciation that everyone had something to bring to the table, some skill to share.

"What do you remember about the McCampbell twins when we were back in school?" Fergie asked him.

"Not much."

"Did you ever date either of them?"

"Oh my, no. They were way out of my league."

"Did you ever hear anything about them?" Al asked.

"Like what?"

"I don't know, that one of them was different?"

"You mean like an evil twin?"

"Yeah. That's the kind of thing I had in mind." Al watched the corner of Fergie's mouth twist up, but she'd probably been thinking the same thing.

"I think all that was just some locker-room-fantasy stuff going around. Evil twin." He laughed as he swung the saddle up onto Bob's back. "But if you really want insight on that score, you should ask Colin. He's been married to both of them and was seeing them both at the same time for a spell, if we're allowed to speak out of school."

As they swung up into their saddles, Wes looked up at them. "What do you hope to accomplish?"

"We don't know yet," Al admitted, "but doing something, anything, feels better than sitting around on our tender rumps waiting for the local law and such to stir into more action than a frog sitting on a stump."

They kept the horses to a walk for the first few hundred yards to get their feel for riding again. Fergie said, "It's funny how some people can go through life in the same rut where they started."

"Are you talking about Wes?"

She nodded.

"I don't know. There's always a lot more to know about people than you get in just a few minutes of chatting."

"Yeah. You're right. He might have left that old rut... and is in a whole new rut by now." She gave her horse a couple of clicks and took Bob up to a trot. Without being asked, Ol' Sal fell into a matching gait.

Al tried to savor the ride out across the property, taking in a pair of scissor-tail flycatchers rising from the tall grass to grab at insects, the steers grazing in the distance, and an occasional wildflower willing to brave the heat of the sun.

They came at last to a gate at the back corner of Meryl's property. The gate was locked, but the lock was on a chain Al could lift off a post and set aside until they were through. He slipped the chain back into place.

It felt a little daring to be riding the horses off the property. He didn't know whose property they were on, but the spread over the fence to their left was the one that interested them. It looked to be just sweeping hills of buffalo grass so far.

The sun was heating up in earnest, and they hadn't dressed for that. Al wore a dark-blue shirt, and Fergie had on a black blouse. Fergie took some sunblock lotion out of her pack, and they both rubbed some on their ears, since they still wore ball caps. Fergie had gone without her usual Smith & Wesson Chief's Special in an ankle holster, since they would probably be doing some hiking.

They sat their horses in the gravel and rocks of the wash Cricket had said ran along inside and under the lip of the mesa. Al could see it tapering out in the distance ahead. They had only so much farther, and they would be in thick growth.

"The severed finger does sound like the Maras," Fergie said. "It's their style."

"I don't like that it wasn't cut very cleanly, the way a machete would do it."

"But still, a finger?"

"Yeah. Whoever did that knew how to press the right buttons. I thought Meryl was going to lose her lunch. I guess she's taken to her bed."

"Maybe because Colin still has no intention of forking over five hundred thousand."

"Would you give up that kind of money for a son?" Al asked.

"If I had it and if I had a son. The rub could be that Baron is only a stepson to Colin."

"I'm sorry I said that about a son. I know you would have liked to have had children."

"Forget about it. I'm over that, mostly." She looked away, and he gave her a few moments to mull over whatever was on her mind.

Al led the way along open stretches of gravel and flat rocks. The day was plenty warm enough for rattlesnakes to be active, so he watched out for them.

He stayed to the right, hugging the rise in gravel and rock that led up to a gradually higher mesa. They came across occasional patches of plants in thick, thorny clumps.

After they had ridden for half a mile or so, the wash began to peter out as the vegetation took over. "We'd better leave the horses here. There's a patch of shade that's growing where they'll be okay for a spell."

While he was still on the mare's back, Al took out his binoculars and looked across the spread to their left, scanning everything within range.

"How far do we need to go in?" Fergie asked. She tied Bob's reins to the same dead mesquite tree where Al had tied Ol' Sal, not too close together so each could still bend to get at some bunch grass.

"I have no idea. Maybe we'll get lucky, and everything will be way back on this end of the spread."

"Why do I doubt that?" She shifted her backpack and took off after Al.

"I did catch a glimpse of something. The land's pretty flat on this side, though the ranch is hillier farther in."

"What did you see?"

"Let's wait and see when we get closer. I didn't know quite what to make of it."

About half the plants in Texas were ready to prick Al with their stickers or at least stick to him. He was running into more than his share of these and paused now and again to rub at a puncture on his thigh or scrape beggar's lice and such off his pants. But when he looked back, Fergie was pulling a cactus needle out of her shin without complaining, so that kept him moving silently ahead.

At last, they topped a small rise and came to what Al had seen.

A wide, flat dirt lane bisected the pasture. Even the buffalo grass had been cut away, and all the stands of cacti and scrub bush were gone. Al guessed it had taken several hands and quite a few days with a Bobcat to make it.

"It's an air field, a landing strip," Fergie said.

"And out as far into the middle of Bumfart Nowhere as you can get."

"What do you suppose they're getting in or sending out from way out here?" Fergie asked.

"We're not going to find out here." Al couldn't see so much as a wind sock. The strip was just an open flat wound in the earth. He took off walking in the direction where he hoped to find some buildings, ones that could hold Baron.

On the other side of the pasture, they came across parallel ruts that led off into the gentle hills. They started walking.

They'd gone only a mile or so when the sound of engines coming toward them caused Al to grab Fergie's upper arm and point to the only stand of thicker brush near them.

She nodded and followed closely, even when Al broke into a near run.

Just as they tucked themselves behind the bit of cover, a line of five gators—green, open-top utility vehicles—pulling small trailers piled high rolled into sight. They moved slowly, since most of the men walked beside or behind the gators. Quite a few of the men clustered near the first one. When Al zoomed in on it with his binoculars, he could see why. Big brick-like plastic squares were clear enough for Al to see that they contained bills, probably hundreds. The other trailers were piled high with boxes of retail merchandise of the kind that might come from hijacked trucks.

"Well, there's one piece of the puzzle," Fergie whispered.

"Still leaves a lot of questions unanswered," Al whispered back.

They were close enough that Al could see every detail of their caravan clearly. He counted men.

"Forty," Fergie whispered, which tallied with what he'd gotten.

Most of the men looked very young—teenagers, maybe early twenties at most. Only a few were heavily tattooed.

One young man plodded along at the front of the group. The lead gator slowed to a stop.

"*Aquí?*" someone yelled from it.

The front figure stopped. Al watched him shrug.

Three men got out of the front vehicle and came up to the solitary young fellow. They led him in the direction where Al and Fergie were hiding. They ducked lower but kept their binoculars fixed on the small group.

Abruptly, the fellow they were escorting dropped to his knees.

The others stood to one side except the most tattooed one of them. He came close and yelled a few things in Spanish too rapidly for Al to catch, though he did pick up on the words "*pendejo*" and "*cabrón*."

At a yelled order, the young man on his knees held out his hands in front of him.

The man with the machete swung it up then down hard. He chopped and chopped until one hand fell off into the high grass on the ground. Each hand took several machete blows to separate from the arm and fall. The young man just knelt there, staring at his hands as it happened. Al could see the first red stub pulsing out two streams of blood in spurts timed to the man's heartbeat, which was rapid. Chop, chop, chop, and the other hand fell off.

Al wanted to lower his binoculars, but he couldn't. He was mesmerized. The face of the young man showed no pain, just quiet acceptance. He kept his head down, staring at where his hands had been and where his life's blood was pulsing out of his body. That was the hardest to take, the young man's accepting stare at the pulsing stubs of his own arms. Al swung his glasses to the others, expecting them to step closer and render some aid. They didn't.

He looked at the faces of the men who still stood in place by the halted caravan. They neither smiled nor frowned, though one or two nodded.

When he looked back, the man with no hands slumped then fell onto his side. Two of the men stepped closer. Each grabbed a leg, and they began to drag the guy toward the clump of brush behind which Al and Fergie hid. Al saw the fallen man's stubs of arms rise once or twice, finally falling to his sides as the men dragged him the rest of the way. They let go of him when he was beside the brush.

Al and Fergie pressed all the way to the ground.

They heard the caravan begin to move again but waited until they could no longer hear it before they looked up. The last of the men and vehicles were out of sight.

They eased around to look down at the young man who lay on the ground. They could do nothing for him. He had bled out, and it would be up to the coyotes and buzzards to take care of what was left. Not even a burial, Al thought, and somewhere the young man had parents, a father and mother who were wondering about him, perhaps worrying. They would never know.

"Thirty-nine of them now," Fergie said.

"Do you think this is some kind of training camp for recruits?" Al looked ahead to where the caravan had gone.

"Sure seems that way. And apparently, the penalty for stealing is pretty harsh. They teach their lessons firmly."

Al didn't have anything to add to that. He started to lead the way back. The going was slower. They were both tired and more than a little emotionally drained.

As soon as he suspected they were getting close to the airstrip, Al led the way to the far right, behind some slight hills where they could make their way around without being seen. It took an hour or two until they were on the far side of the airstrip and heading toward the fence they'd climbed to enter the spread. The sun was sliding over the horizon in a splash of red and orange, pink and purple.

Shadows crept out from the few trees and the occasional low bluff. The sky began to darken in earnest.

They paused for a moment to drink from their canteens. Fergie glanced toward the stretch ahead. "Maybe we should have gone up onto the mesa, where we could see more and perhaps not get stuck in the dark."

"We would have missed that delightful scene that's going to haunt a dream or two," Al said.

They took off walking again, using every scrap of cover to stay out of sight.

Al could still see fairly well, though the shadows were growing. Soon, they would be feeling their way along, which was not the best way to move through a harsh land full of stickers and who-knew-what critters.

The light had faded almost completely by the time Al heard shouts from behind them. At first, he thought they'd been spotted even as they were almost to the fence. He held out a hand to hold Fergie still.

They looked back, but Al couldn't see anyone coming their way. When he lifted his binoculars, he could see activity. Men were setting out lights along the edges of the small runway.

Al couldn't see a hangar anywhere, just an airfield in the middle of the flattest part of the land.

They stood still. Al heard the beginning of a buzz in the distance. He looked up at the sky, which was black with only a sprinkling of stars showing. The sound grew louder. He watched for a plane's lights but didn't see any.

"I don't understand," Fergie said. "I thought the days of planes flying under the radar were gone."

"Apparently this pilot hasn't gotten the word, and he's good."

"How can you tell?"

"Because he's flying without lights."

?

Emile la Rogue was a name the lone pilot had come up with when he left commercial airlines behind. He could have flown for any of them and had even turned down an offer to fly for Emirates Airlines, where he could have retired with a pension. But the money he made was much better, and he kind of enjoyed the thrill of any risk. He could fly any of the Sinaloa cartel's planes, and they had their own air force. A Cessna, he could fly wearing a blindfold—or in this case, without the lights on. He quite liked it in the dark sky, alone with the dash lights and the humming low roar of the engine, the treetops skimming by close beneath the small plane.

He began his descent, waiting until the last moment to flip on the lights and splash a glare onto the makeshift runway. The cartel maintained over five thousand such airstrips, and the schedule was never the same, never predictable. The cartel had used planes more sparingly since the Mexican government had confiscated over 600 planes of all sizes over a ten-year period. But business being business, there were always more planes.

He bounced along the runway, slowing as quickly as he could, cursing whoever had left a few potholes big enough to lift him off his seat a couple of times.

As soon as he stopped, men came swarming out to unload. There were other, safer ways to get the crates of rifles and the special part of this load to the clique of men—by truck, for instance. But the push was on to train new recruits if they were ever to claw back parts of Houston from those Los Zetas-backed Tango Blast gangsters who'd kicked MS-13 out of the Bayou City. That needed to happen as soon as possible.

He kept an eye on his watch. Six minutes down, less than nine minutes to go. When they had the crates of M-16s as well as the urgently needed special crates that had necessitated the flight unloading, they started to bring boxes of merchandise toward the plane. "Hey. No!" he shouted out his window. "You keep that merch. Sell it back door to the convenience stores. I don't want loaded down with that crap. You got cash bundles. I'll take those."

The load going back onto the plane was smaller and took less time.

"Tick. Tick. Tick," he yelled. "I'm taking off now."

They slammed the hatches and doors shut. He turned the plane and took off. As soon as he was up over the treetops again, he doused the lights. People across his path in their little farmhouses could wake and hear a sound, but if they looked up, they would see nothing. Maybe they would think he was a big bug. He chuckled to himself.

?

As the plane lifted off the ground with its lights on for a moment, the beams swept across Al and Fergie, just about blinding them.

Fergie blinked and watched the plane rise. Its lights abruptly went off, and it seemed to disappear except for the sound of its engine.

She felt relief for only a second or two. Then she heard shouts.

"Someone's up there! Did you see them?"

"Claro que sí."

Even with the lights of the plane no longer spotlighting them, shots began to pour at them from below. Visibility had to be far from perfect, but with so many people shooting rounds from automatic weapons at them, the chance of someone getting lucky was high.

Al could hear leaves being shredded from the low trees and brush around them as they crouched and scooted along as fast as they could go.

In the occasional brief pauses between flurries of shooting, Al could see lights from the gators bouncing across the field toward them. He could hear the shouts and imagined the sounds of men tearing through brush as they came after them. He ran as fast as he could, barely keeping up with Fergie and her ridiculously long legs.

She turned to him as she ran. "Do you recall what Satchel Paige once said?"

"Yeah." Al panted. "He said, 'Don't look back. Something might be gaining on you.' And it seems like he was onto something. That's a helluva good idea at the moment."

Chapter Thirteen

S hots whizzed past their ducked heads as they ran flat-out. Above the sounds of their boots crunching on gravel and slapping against flat rock, he could hear the gators get to the edge of the fence and could imagine the swarms of gun-wielding and machete-bearing men pouring over the fence behind them.

Even with Fergie's longer legs to vie against, Al was right at her side as they went at a full run up the wash and toward where they'd left the horses. He remembered the sight of blood pumping out of that young man's severed wrists until what life was left in him just went away, and that kept his feet moving faster than usual.

As much as he would have liked to pause and catch his breath, he swung up into the saddle as soon as he reached the horses. Fergie had already jerked her reins free and had turned Bob to head back the way they'd come.

Al didn't think he could get Ol' Sal up to a full gallop, but she got there herself by trying to keep up with Bob, who was no doubt inspired by the sound of bullets ricocheting off the rocks dotting the dirt wall along the base of the mesa.

The darkness all around them covered their escape but kept them from seeing anything. At least the horses knew where they were going.

Just as he was thinking that, Ol' Sal clipped a rock with her hoof and nearly stumbled. But bless her old heart, she regained her footing and rhythm and kept pace with galloping Bob.

As the sounds of heavy automatic gunfire faded behind them the faster they went, Al felt around, surprised that not a single shot had clipped him anywhere. Ol' Sal seemed as untouched, and she was inspired to run. He listened to the steady clopping of her shod hooves on the stone and gravel of the wash. She maintained her flat-out gallop until Fergie pulled up ahead of him at the gate that went into the back end of Meryl's spread.

Panting, Al eased closer. "Are you okay?"

"Except for my heart having a race with itself, I'm fine." She was breathing hard, too, although the horses had done the real getaway work. "Thank heaven the fastest of those after us back there were young recruits who probably couldn't hit a bunkhouse from a dozen feet away."

"They were enthusiastic enough, though," Al said.

She lowered the gate chain back into place behind them. "Something's sure going on. We just don't know what."

They sat their horses for a moment or two and listened. Al could hear no sign of them being followed. Taking off in the dark as they had might have left the Maras with no clear idea of which way they had gone. The shooting in their direction had certainly not been tightly focused.

"We know a little more than we did, but it's not much," Al said, "and we saw no sign of Baron."

"Does that mean we have to go back in there?"

"Almost certainly. But maybe we can use stealth. I doubt they would expect us to revisit."

"I don't know. I've seen hornet's nests knocked to the ground that were less stirred up than those guys." She started Bob off at a slow walk so they could talk. "Do you think drugs are involved?"

Al turned to start Ol' Sal back across the spread to Meryl's ranch house. "I don't think so. It might be about that in the future, since a cartel is probably behind this. But with what looks like young recruits being armed and trained, it's about something else—maybe power."

"You think there's going to be a war?"

"Maybe. But with whom?" Al asked. "We do know one thing."

"What's that?"

"That if Baron is in that place, he's in the middle of some sense of urgency from these guys about whatever's going to happen."

"Yep, and it's probably something we don't want to be any part of."

"But we may have to be if we're to get him free."

"I sure wish there was some other way." She gave Bob a nudge with her heels and picked up the pace, heading him home.

?

Fergie watched Al lead Ol' Sal to the stable door and give her a pat on the rump to send her out into the corral.

"I believe a few more days in the saddle, and you're going to turn into a seasoned cowhand," she said.

"Tell that to my hindquarters." Al glanced out into the corral. "But that old mare sure delivered today. Without her, I'd hate to think what kind of hamburger those Maras would have made out of us."

"I just hope the darkness of night covered any notion of 'they went thataway.' I doubt if they even got a clear look at us." She turned Bob out and carried his reins over to the racks on the wall.

"I wish we could talk to your pal Jaime Avila. He and his ICE friends could maybe explain what Maras are doing out at a nowhere ranch."

"Maybe. But the thing about opening a line of communication with Jaime is closing it. And he would tell us to just go home while he takes over."

"Maybe that wouldn't be altogether a bad thing," she said.

As they were putting the tack away, Meryl came in and watched them for a moment. "I need to speak with you two."

"It's going to have to top being shot at by your neighbors, who we can now confirm are Mara Salvatruchas. About forty of them are pretty fussed up at the moment." Al swung his saddle onto its stand.

"Thirty-nine." Fergie shook her head.

"Oh, yeah. We saw them murder one of their own—bled him out by chopping off his hands, probably for stealing."

Meryl quivered almost delicately. "I so thought life out here was going to be peaceful this far away from cities and all that's going on there."

Even in the dim light of a lone bulb hanging from a wire, she looked far too attractive for Fergie to believe Meryl was their age. She wondered for a moment how Ferrill had looked. Probably as good. *It must be in the genes.*

"I was hoping you might speak to Colin."

"And get him to do what?"

"Just pay the ransom and get this behind us."

"Why hasn't he?"

"Well, for one, it's not his son. It's mine. But the story he tells is about the tangle his money needs to stay in if it is to produce. It needs to be let alone to grow."

"A half million would affect him that much?"

"That's in his head. If it was me, and I had his money, I'd just pay up and not look back."

"He won't do it for Baron?"

"He won't do it for *me.*"

Fergie shook her head. "What the two of us need right now is a little rest."

"Do you think—?"

"Yep. We have to go back over there."

"Didn't you say the place was filled with the nastiest sort of people?"

Fergie shrugged. "I said I'd try to find Baron, and until we do, I won't give up."

"So you won't speak to Colin... about the money?"

"If he won't listen to you, I'm sure he wouldn't pay me any attention," Fergie said. "You're far more attractive than me."

"Why... thank you. I think."

Fergie and Al were almost to the stable door when Meryl spoke again.

"Maybe you should look in on Baron's friends Darren and Dewey again. Didn't you say you got very little in the way of help from them?"

Chapter Fourteen

Mauricio watched Gino and José opening the crates and taking out the M-16s. They were packed covered in Cosmoline and plastic bags, just like in the old days. He'd have a crew of the *chequeos* use kerosene for what couldn't be wiped off with rags. Then the guns would be ready for action. Two of the wooden cases contained ammo, which he was glad to see. They were going to be ready at last, after much preparation.

"Leave those cases there alone for now." Mauricio pointed at the boxes of grenades. Not all of the recruits had ironed out their shooting yet, and he planned to save the grenades for the coming confrontation in the city. They were going to rock Houston up onto its end. "And those as well. Leave them be for now." He pointed to the wooden crates marked "MANPADS." Maybe he, Isaác, and a couple or three of the others were ready and could use the contents of those boxes. But he didn't trust the others with what was inside, not yet. That would probably need to happen before the great city confrontation to come.

Their row of gators had been parked in a line against the unlit far wooden wall of the barnlike structure that must have once housed goats, given its smell. The barracks or bunkhouse next to it didn't smell much better, but the recruits didn't complain, and there were no young *chicas* to offend. Isaác stood close with a clipboard, keeping tally. They'd been lucky to get their hands on so many M-16s. He was used to the older guns, and they were cheaper than the newer ones. They were fine for training a *clica* like his.

He caught Gino stealing envious glances at Isaác's tats. Gino was one to watch. Mauricio had told them no more ink for now. When they got back to Houston, he wanted them to fit in and be invisible, not display out-and-out threats.

He could see where Gino had taken some ink and a pin and had started his own homemade tat on the web of his left hand between the thumb and forefinger. That was how prison tattoos looked, and Gino had to like that a lot too. Three dots in a triangular formation formed the symbol for *la vida loca*, the crazy life of a gangbanger. The three dots meant the wearer expected to end up in a hospital, in prison, or dead—simple as that.

Isaác, who at twenty-three years old was the second oldest in the clica under Mauricio, may only have been five foot three and one hundred forty-one pounds, but he claimed to have been in over a hundred fistfights, knife fights, gun battles, and drive-bys. He had a tattooed flag of El Salvador on his stomach and a three-inch-high MS-13 on his left shoulder.

"We be ready for the *chavala* soon," Isaác said. "The enemy," he added after a quick glance from Mauricio for using Spanish.

"I want to know about last night some more. You, Gino, what you think you see?" Mauricio turned to the young *chequeo*.

"I don' know. Could a been those two guys wit' the meth lab. I din' get a real good look."

"I think you just want to hit a meth lab," Mauricio said.

"Is not a bad idea. Lots of times, you find money at these places," Isaác said. "They can't—*cómo se dice*, how you say it?—take it to the laundry."

"Maybe we could clean that money for them," Gino said.

José nodded. Like the other young recruits, he probably welcomed the chance for some real action, not just shooting at targets and running about.

"How are we on weapons and ammo?" Mauricio asked, knowing the answer in advance but just wanting to hear it.

Isaác grinned. "We got plenty. Plenty enough, tha's for sure. I'd hate to see the *cholos* we come across right now wit' what we got."

"I'll be right back." Mauricio walked out of the barn's wide main room. He paused just outside the door and listened for a moment.

"Where's he going?" Gino asked.

"Probably gotta check with his playmaker," Isaác said.

"All the way back in El Salvador?"

"Probably."

"How's he do it? Call or internet?" Gino asked.

"I don't ask, 'cause I don' wanna know. When you run your own *clica*, you'll know." Isaác stood up and headed for the door.

As soon as he came blinking out into the brighter sunlight, Mauricio said, "Psst."

Isaác came over to stand close.

"I miss the old days when we drove about, shooting out the windows of cars," Mauricio said. "Maybe Gino has the right idea."

"Don' you need to check with someone abou' somethin'?"

"Naw." Mauricio waited a tick then grinned. "My bosses are disappointed we didn't get at least a hunnert new recruits, say it'll take at least that to carve back our place in Houston with them Tango Blast bangers trying to stop us. They say we oughta have at least fifty new members if we can't get a hunnert."

"Now, we don't got even forty," Isaác said. "Only one way to get them bosses to think less about that: money."

"You right about that. What I hear is always the same. If there's money in it, do it. Sometimes, I think we just a business, not bangers no more."

Isaác nodded. "Way out here, we can't shake down no *Mexicanos* without papers or sell *chicas* or nothing fun."

"You telling me," Mauricio said. "We got just two jobs right now. Get these new recruits ready for battle and get cash wherever and however we can."

"We could knock over tha' meth lab I hear about. You see, at the same time we training the *chequeos* and making money, too, maybe even get some danger and fun in that."

Mauricio grinned. He was sure enough tired of the youngsters just running around and playing practice games. "Well, what the hell then, *amigo*? Let's go get ready for that. Then *vámanos.*"

?

Al headed down the wooden stairs by himself, giving Fergie a little time and space to herself for the kind of daily prep in front of a mirror she liked to take her time doing.

The sun was up, but the day was not nearly as hot as it could get.

He watched a bobbing figure in the distance, a lone runner coming up the lane toward the house. As the man got nearer, Al could make out that it was Colin, dressed in a gray tank top, dark-blue running shorts, and sneakers that looked thick and oversized.

Colin saw Al and slowed to a stop. He wore a blue Houston Astros baseball cap instead of his straw cowboy hat. Their gang colors were blue and white, and the Maras from Houston were called "Houstones." They sometimes wore Astros caps or had tattoos of the logo, too, and Al wondered if Colin knew he might accidentally be wearing gang colors. While on the sheriff's department, Al had figured out the cause of one drive-by hit of an innocent victim. He just happened to be wearing the wrong color bandana hanging out of his back pocket and died never knowing there was a whole bandana code out there in the seamy world few fully understood.

"Out having a jog to keep fit?" Al asked.

"You bet. What with Gaby's good cooking, I have to work to stay the kind of guy able to attract two trophy wives, the kind nobody thinks were for second place." He chuckled.

Al didn't have a snappy response to that.

"How are you guys coming along with finding Baron?" Colin asked. "The regular law enforcement around here sure isn't making any headway."

"We're doing all we can and nosing about in the mysterious ways we usually use to perform our wonders." Al glanced up the stairs to see if Fergie had emerged yet.

"That's vague."

"This case is vague, so far. But we aim to clear it up."

"Well, I sure hope you get a move on."

Al tilted his head a quarter inch to the right. "What outcome do you hope for here?"

"That Fergie can find Baron and get him back home as soon as possible."

"Before you have to pay any ransom?"

"Oh, that's not happening no matter what."

"Does Meryl know your stand on that?"

"Of course."

"I'll bet you're having some swell times together."

"Tell you the truth, it's better when she's mad."

"Was she mad at her sister when you two were sneaking off together while you were still married to Ferrill?"

"You heard about that?"

"Yeah."

"You wouldn't understand."

"Why so?"

Colin seemed to be considering something and finally went ahead and said it. "Do you know what Meryl told me?"

"No. What?"

"That you and Fergie were voted the worst couple at your senior prom, the most unlikely ever to have another date."

"And?"

"And here you are, together after all these years. I didn't expect to get you in the bargain when I asked Fergie for help."

"Yet here I am."

"And you're flailing away. I do hope you two grab some traction and get this solved."

"You do realize that we're working for free here, don't you?"

"That's the way I prefer to hire help," Colin said. "Fergie probably explained that to you. I'm a bit of a cheapskate."

Colin spun and started to jog away. He was just going out of sight around the ranch house when Fergie came out the door of their luxury suite and started down the stairs.

Al was still staring off at nothing, so she asked, "What are you mulling over so intensely?"

"I was thinking over our happy high-school days."

"Oh, you shouldn't do that."

"Let me ask you a prying personal question. How did you come to date a bit of pond scum like Colin and agree to help him?"

Her mouth turned up at one corner. "I would suggest that you dated the occasional frog or toad, but I now know too much of your story. After your military experience, your brief college days whirled by, since it took you only three years to get your degree because you and the G.I. Bill were paying all of your own way. Then you married Abbie, had the horrible experience with your brother Maury and her, and then you went into a hole and never dated again. Until now."

"Why help Colin?" Al persisted.

"Because since hooking up with you—I believe that's how it's put these days—I've grown an appreciation for making my life useful with the skills I possess by sometimes helping people, even those who no one else would otherwise help."

"Oh."

"And if you ask what keeps me going in this particular case, after being reacquainted with Colin's particular pond scumminess, it's coming our way right now."

Al turned to look where she was staring. Cricket was headed their way. Her fine blond hair fluttered in the breeze, and Al could see a dimple on one round cheek. She stopped when she got to them and looked up at them. "How are you coming along at finding my dad?"

"We're working hard at it," Fergie said, "and we're about to ride off on that mission again today."

"Well, I sure wish you well and hope for a speedy success. I'm starting to get right worried. Everyone is acting strange about this. He's left me in Gaby's care a time or two before while he was off to attend to one thing or another, but he's never been gone so long. The sheriff's acting funny, and Auntie Gran and Colin are too. No one tells me anything."

"As soon as we know anything," Fergie said, "you're the first person we're going to think of telling. Okay?"

"Just do your best." Cricket struggled for a smile but didn't stick its landing. A tear started down her dimpled cheek.

Chapter Fifteen

Baron sat on the straight-backed chair with no choice about the matter at all. His wrists were taped tightly in place behind the chair's back, and his ankles were still taped to the chair's legs. He couldn't wiggle the chair the least bit with his feet, so he certainly had no way of doing that film or television stunt of hopping around enough to knock the chair over on its side to break it into kindling. A stretch of the silver duct tape also crossed his mouth from one cheek to the other, clinging to the stubble that had grown since he hadn't been able to shave.

His little finger, or the place where the finger should have been, tingled. They'd taped the wound, but the spot had throbbed for a while. Try as he might to make a joke, maybe that he wouldn't ever play the piano again, he couldn't. Seeing what Darren and Dewey were capable of had opened his eyes and scared him as he'd never been scared before.

The door to the cabin opened, and Darren came through. Dewey followed, carrying a platter of ribs.

"I'll tell you one thing, you cook up a mean rib," Darren said. "We had a brief taste. You might could have used a bit more dry rub, but you made do with what you had out here. We brung along some sauce, so we'll be fine. I sure wish you could have a taste. But you know how that is."

"Water!" Baron tried to say. It came out as a muffled "mwa mwa" from behind the tape.

Darren tilted his head, but Dewey seemed to understand. He took a small bottle of water out of the fridge, pulled the tape away from Baron's mouth, and poured in about a third of the bottle before stopping. In a smooth motion, he had the tape back in place before Baron could say a word.

"Be careful with that water, Dewey, or you'll have him needing to go to the bathroom."

"Too late," Dewey said as he glanced down at Baron's jeans. He walked back toward the table and sat down across from Darren. He reached for one of the ribs.

"Mmm. Wish you could taste this." Darren chewed at a bite from the rib he held. He waved it for Baron to see.

Baron wanted to scream, "Why? Why? Why? I thought you guys were my friends." All he could do was mumble from behind the tape.

"I do wish you could join us. I truly do," Darren said. "But you see, when your hay fields and such burned up, you weren't the only one who took a financial setback. Right, Dewey? Tell him."

"That Mary Jane patch was ours. Had to put gasoline on it and burn it down, fast."

"You see, we got a tip that the law had found it and were heading out to take care of it, make some arrests. What else could we do?"

"And..." Dewey managed to say in spite of a mouthful of beef rib.

"Oh, yeah. The business with Julie Ann," Darren said. "You should know that once you two got married, neither of us had anything to do with her... until *after* Cricket was born."

"So it's more than likely she's your kid." Dewey wiped his mouth with a piece of paper towel.

"I will say you grew some mighty good beef. This isn't the first of it we've tasted the past few years." Darren dropped one bare rib bone on the plate and reached for a meaty one.

"Yeah, when the deer gave out, you pretty much helped us get by. We were lucky you never kept the kind of close count that I'll bet Meryl is keeping."

"Yeah, she's a hard one for a deal. But once in a while, she comes up a cropper, and this just might be her time." Dewey chuckled at a joke Baron didn't get.

Baron wanted to ask why they were bothering to keep him alive. But even if his mouth wasn't taped shut, he was scared of the answer he might get.

"You never really asked," Darren said, "but Dewey and me were best friends from the time we were in middle school. There were those who picked on us individually, but together, we were far better off. Some of those who'd had an easy time with us when we were by ourselves got pretty surprised later in the nights when the two of us got *our* chance."

"It all kind of taught us to be meaner than anyone but to just not let anyone know about that."

"Yeah, it was us against the world," Darren said, "and no one caught on until it was too late for them."

Baron shivered and struggled for a moment against the tape. He sure wished they weren't being so candid about everything. That wasn't a good sign for him, not a good sign at all.

Baron tried again to scream at them, "I never bullied you. Why are you doing this to me?" But everything he tried to say was muffled by the tape.

Dewey put the bones they'd picked clean into a paper bag. He stood up and headed for the door.

"I think we cheered him up some," Darren said as he followed him across the room.

"That's good. He seemed a little down."

?

As soon as they were outside the cabin, Dewey carried the beef-rib bones over to the deer fence only eighty-five yards on the other side of the cabin.

The previous owners, bless them, had put up the eight-foot-high fence all around the spread back during its prosperous days. Dewey wasn't sure whether it was to keep the deer out or in. But the deer hunting was darn puny after the first few years of his and Darren's living in the place, so he guessed it was to keep them out.

He started to throw the rib bones over the fence one by one, letting them land in dull, thudding plops in the high grass and open stretches of dirt on the other side. "That'll give you varmint coyotes something to fuss over."

As he got back to the front of the cabin, wiping his hands on his jeans as he went, Darren had the truck running with its side windows open. Dewey climbed in. "Now what?"

"It's time to set up a drop."

"And if they don't go for it?"

"We'll start sending them a finger for each reminder, and we'll keep at that until he's out of fingers and toes. Then we'll start on the other parts of him that come off easy with a bolt cutter."

"Gee, he's sure lucky he's our friend, or it's likely we'd have to go much harder on him," Dewey said.

They both laughed loud and hard as Darren put the truck in gear, and they pulled away.

?

The line of gators pulled up to the gate at the edge of the property. Mauricio hadn't known there was a gate, but Isaác and a crew of the youngest recruits had made daily patrols of the extreme edges of the ranch before they'd started working on the airfield. Mauricio had been after a military-like air among the young men, which was why he'd banned women as well as cell phones and had focused on basic combat skills. He watched them moving as a battle-ready unit and was pleased.

The gate was locked with a rusted padlock on the other side of the eight-foot-high fence. At a wave from Isaác, two of the smallest and most limber of the men scrambled over the fence. One of them trailed a nylon cord behind him. Once they were over, Isaác tied the cutters to the trailing end of the cord, and they pulled the cutters over the top of the fence and dropped them down to them. Mauricio smiled when he heard the tired steel of the padlock separate with a pop.

The gators rolled through the opened gate like a parade. The men not inside the vehicles scattered to the sides to explore and provide cover, though there wasn't a single living thing near them except lizards and an occasionally rattling snake.

Mauricio tried to imagine the young men moving as smoothly and efficiently once they were in the streets of Houston, taking back territory that had belonged to the Maras for a short while.

One of the men who had been out in advance came running back over the top of the gentle hill ahead, waving one arm while carrying his M-16 in the other. As he got closer, Mauricio could see it was José.

He came up to the lead gator and paused while still panting hard. "Cabin. There's a cabin ahead."

"Surround it."

José spun and ran back the way he'd come.

By the time his gator rolled over the rise, the recruits were spread out in a circle, all with rifles pointed at the cabin. Mauricio's gator stopped, and he waved for Isaác to sneak up to the cabin. He and two others crawled just like seasoned marines, holding their rifles across their chests as their elbows and knees took them across the open dirt to the cabin door.

Isaác signaled to the others, and each went to a window to rise quickly and peek inside. They nodded, and Isaác stood, eased up to the door, tried the handle, and then swung it open to look inside. All three rushed inside. In only a moment or two, they came back out and waved to Mauricio. He climbed out of his gator and walked over to the cabin.

Inside, the light was dim in spite of the sunlight struggling in through the grimy windows. He could make out a man tied to a wooden chair with silver duct tape. He glanced to Isaác, who shrugged and shook his head.

Mauricio walked over to the man. "Someone doesn't like you too much, no?" He ripped the tape off the man's mouth.

The man coughed and in a squeaky voice said, "Water?"

Mauricio nodded. Isaác looked around, saw the fridge, and went to it. The only things inside were bottles of water. He reached for the half-empty plastic bottle of water at the front. He carried that over to the tied man and poured it down his throat the way someone might fill their gas tank at a service station.

The man gagged, still gulping at air as Isaác jerked the empty bottle away and tossed it on the floor.

"Name?" Mauricio snapped.

"Baron. Were you looking for me?"

"No, but we finding you, sí?" Mauricio looked around the cabin. He went around the chair once and bent closer when he saw that the little finger was gone from one hand, the spot now covered by a bandage with blood seeping out through the gauze. "Who do this?"

"Some people I thought were friends."

"*Por qué?* Why?"

The man who called himself Baron seemed to think about it and shut his mouth. Mauricio nodded to Isaác, who stepped close and put the duct tape back in place over the man's mouth. His eyes got bigger, and he struggled with the binding that held him to the chair, but Isaác just turned away.

"Leave two men with him, in case we need him for somethin'. Okay?" Mauricio spun on his boot heel and went out the cabin's door.

Outside, the men on foot started off, following the ruts that led away from the cabin. The gators crawled along in the rear echelon position while Isaác had the bulk of the recruits spreading out and using the same approach methods he had planned for the coming confrontations in Houston. Mauricio smiled. He didn't have as many men as he wanted or needed, but add the element of surprise, and he intended to give those Tangoes something to think about.

The slow pace ate up over an hour until they crested a rise, and he could see a weather-worn wooden house below. Isaác and the recruits swarmed into a circular formation and surrounded the house. Mauricio waved to the others to leave the gators and join in the maneuver. The recruits went to the ground and crawled toward the house from all directions.

A lone truck sat parked in front of the long porch that drooped on one end. With the collapsed bunkhouse and bent windmill, the place didn't look like much of a meth lab, but smaller places in trailer parks had served the same purpose. He wouldn't know until they were inside.

Once everyone was in position, Mauricio eased down the hill until he was beside Isaác.

"Now?" Isaác crouched close to the side of the gator where Mauricio sat.

"Give it a minute or two." He was thinking there might be a response. No sense losing men over being hasty. If it was his meth lab, he would have had trip wires set up and a defense plan in place. But with a couple of ranch gringos, it was hard to say. "Look about for any traps, trips, or snares."

He looked up at the sun, which had climbed almost to its zenith in the sky. A lone bird flew along the length of the horizon in the distance. Even the scrap of wind made almost no sound. He waited, squinting at the house.

?

As the other young *chequeos* near José spread out to cover every angle around the farmhouse, with eagerness in their eyes and with their hands probably sweating like his were where they gripped an M-16, he glanced about. Everyone was intently fixed on the structure. Spread out on the dirt, he could feel the grit of it rubbing his knees and elbows and could smell the earthiness of the dusty, dry soil. For the first time, he was as alone as he'd been in days.

José kept an eye on the others as he eased his free hand to his pack. He fumbled for just a moment before slipping out the forbidden burner phone. No women, no phones—the rules had been quite emphatic about that—and no stealing or fighting among themselves.

He swept his eyes across those around him again then held the phone with both hands long enough to turn it on so it could send a signal that could be traced by GPS. He quickly tapped in: "*Aquí.*" Then slipped the phone, still on, back into his pack. That ought to do it, he thought.

They all waited. He stared at the house with the others, but he was seeing Roberto, his brother, as his hands fell off and his life's blood pulsed out of him from his wrists in six-inch spurts. José had been one of those who'd been ordered to grab a leg and pull Roberto toward the brush to leave him there.

As he'd been dragged along, Roberto had lifted the bleeding stubs of his arms toward José, whether for one last hug or to ask for help. Then his eyes had dimmed, and the arms dropped to drag uselessly along.

José had told him not to steal, however tempting it might have been. What good was money, out where they were? But Roberto had slipped the tip of his knife into one of the shrink-wrapped bundles of hundreds and had tugged out just a few of the bills, barely a couple thousand.

Their father had been in prison for most of their growing-up years, but he was out and was Puro Tango Blast. He was coming José's way, and when he found out about Roberto, he was going to be pretty pissed off. He would understand the rules of the banger life, but all the same, José expected he would be pretty darn pissed off. *Muy enojado!*

Chapter Sixteen

"I'm trying to think what it would be like to be a twin when one of you dies," Fergie said. Her breath came in huffs, since she was carrying the saddle to swing it onto the blanket on Bob's back. "Would it feel like half of you is gone?"

She reached under to get the end of the cinch, slipped it through the buckle, and pulled it tight. She waited a moment for Bob to take a breath then pulled the cinch tighter. By golly, a week or two of this and they would be regular hands, if their sore rears held out.

"Maybe that's only something you'd know if you'd been a twin," Al said.

"I suppose. It just seems they have a special relationship with their sibling that way. Though I never even had a sibling."

"I did. For a long stretch there, you could have had Maury with no argument from me."

"Back to Colin. Why do you suppose he'd marry both twins?"

"Maybe he got in the habit of looking at one and didn't want to stray from the pattern too much."

Fergie shook her head. "If the mumbling around the campfire has anything to it, he got a bit of a jump on the second marriage while still married to Ferrill. Where would Colin see the charm in that?"

"You're asking the wrong guy. I'm more drawn to those one-of-a-kind gals."

"Oh, get off it." But Fergie had felt a warm tingle as he'd said it.

"I was in on a raid on one of those gentlemen's dance clubs, the kind where clothing is very optional for the dancers. We burst inside, and twenty young, stark-naked blond girls were up dancing on the tables. Their identical bodies were the athletic-cheerleader type, and their faces and hairdos were alike. They must have been recruited because they all looked exactly the same. It felt like a room filled with twins."

"Did that move you?"

"No," he said. "I don't know when I've ever been less turned on."

"Must've seemed like a machine was cloning them. I think I can understand." Fergie was looking around at the inside of the stable. The wood of the walls and floor was solid, the floor was swept clean, and all the gear was neatly in its proper places. Some of that spoke of Wes's military background. His efforts complemented the solid and nice-though-not-fancy buildings on the spread.

There wasn't much to the ranch. Raising cattle and hay should have been a booming enterprise, even with a setback or two. It probably was, now that Meryl owned it. Fergie struggled to figure out how it had all gotten away from Baron, and now he was missing on top of that. All except a finger. They had that.

While he was saddling up Ol' Sal, Al paused and looked at Fergie. "We're not going to do the sensible thing here and stop, are we?"

"No. But you tell me why."

"Because we started it," he said.

"I've seen you on a case before. It's why you had the best detective record in the sheriff's department."

"Even for someone the likes of Colin?"

"You know we're not doing it for him at this point. And you know who we are doing it for."

"Of course." He checked his cinch again, making sure he'd pulled it as tight as he could.

She led her horse out of the barn, and Al followed with Ol' Sal. As soon as they were outside, she swung herself up into the saddle.

He swung himself up, too, but added an "oompf."

As they started off, Fergie rode beside him. "Does your behind still hurt? Notice I'm trying not to say 'butt' all the time."

"Of course it does. I suppose there wasn't a single cowhand in all the west who thought, 'I know what: foam padding.' No, they just had to sit on something hard as a board all day long."

They rode slowly at first.

"Do you ever wonder how it would have been if you and I had gotten together sooner and been that way longer?" Fergie glanced his way.

"First of all, I don't think it would have worked at all. We both hadn't had enough of the sharp edges knocked off yet. Now, maybe we have. Even more importantly, I try never to regret anything. Life isn't about do-overs. It's about being in the moment."

"Well then, let's ride out into our moment today and hope it isn't our last one."

They picked up the pace and were soon moving at a steady gait across the spread. The cattle grazed, and the wind kicked up waves across the flowing hills of golden hay. At any other time, she would have enjoyed the ride instead of thinking ahead to the sort of people they might come close to again. But it had to be done.

She slowed Bob to a careful walk through a stretch of the pasture where she'd seen what looked like prairie dog holes, although they could have been from armadillos, skunks, or just about anything that burrowed. She didn't want Bob to step in one and hurt a hoof or worse.

Al glanced her way. "Maybe the attraction thing with Colin and Meryl is simpler than we're making it out to be. He was used to living with someone, and so was she. They each lost that someone."

"And they had had a little practice at playing house, anyway," Fergie said.

"I think money might've been a factor too. Did you find him a little more attractive when you found out he had some?"

Ol' Sal took advantage of the slower pace and grabbed at a mouthful of bunch grass. Bob did the same.

"He didn't have quite so much back when we dated, and even that glitter faded when I learned how fond he was of hanging onto it." She eased Bob around a patch of thorny chaparral that led down into an arroyo, a slightly descending groove of a ravine. Fergie shifted in the saddle, feeling Bob's shoulders and haunches moving with each step as he went down a short way then started back up.

When Al didn't say anything for a while, she poked at the fire again. "What makes you an expert on the likes of either of them wanting to remarry? Does that come from your years of living alone?"

"Hey, I was married once."

"Briefly enough, before Maury threw a spanner wrench into that."

"Some of the blame there belongs to Abbie and maybe a little to me. I really did expect to sail through the following years by myself."

"But...?"

He gave her a sideways look. "But I've enjoyed the time you and I have had together. Even little outings like this one."

"Even when they came close to getting us killed a few times?"

"That wasn't the objective, but I can't say it didn't add zest and encourage me to savor the times we have when we've made it."

"We did just barely make it a time or two."

"But here we are," he said.

"Your life isn't the way you expected."

"Maybe it's better."

Fergie heard hooves pounding behind them and glanced back.

Cricket rode up fast on Diablo. Fergie marveled at how easy and sure the sprightly little gal was in the saddle of the powerful stallion.

Al turned in his saddle to see the girl coming toward them. "You sure had to go the long way 'round to wheedle that out of me."

"Sometimes it takes the long way with you."

Cricket reined the stallion in, and he was blowing hard, the way a good horse would do after a hearty run. "Are you two trying again?" Cricket asked.

"Yeah, and you can't come along," Fergie said.

"Aw. You're about as much fun as my Auntie Gran. 'Don't be such a tomboy.' 'Sit still at the table.' 'Don't squirm so.' It's like she'd rather I was a statue or something."

"Why do you call Meryl your Auntie Gran?"

"She likes it."

"But why?"

"Maybe it's because she's married to my uncle Colin now. Or maybe she doesn't want me feeling too close... I mean since she's my home-school teacher too. But she's still my gran. Really."

Something in that niggled inside Fergie. It seemed a distancing device that perhaps went with a calculating side to Meryl. Fergie had met women who had a Machiavellian bent, particularly in her days as a city police detective. Anything was possible. A whole lot of years had gone by since being in school with Meryl, and she hadn't known her all that well then.

The wind picked up as they rode until it was coming in gusts that made them hang onto their hats. Cricket took off her cowgirl hat and held it, letting her fine blond hair sweep in short ripples behind her. Fergie looked at the nearest big trees. It was the kind of wind that shook loose the upper dead branches and dropped them to the ground. They were far enough from any of those not to be threatened by falling branches. But she figured it would be one heck of a day to fly a kite.

They got to the gate that led out of Meryl's spread. As Al opened it, Fergie turned to Cricket. "You should stay here."

"Are you kidding? I should at least see where you leave the horses."

That was true enough, though Fergie wondered if that meant in case Al and Fergie didn't make it back. She didn't want to credit the little girl with the kind of experience that could foresee that contingency.

"Okay, just that far. Maybe you could take the horses back to the stable, so they're not out in the wind and sun all day." It was one way to ensure Cricket wouldn't want to tag along, and Fergie *had* begun to worry about the horses in case something happened.

"What about you guys?"

"We'll find a way to get out and back to your place," Fergie said with far more confidence than she felt.

Cricket rode happily along, like they were off to a picnic, until they came to the spot where they'd tied the horses before. They stopped and sat their horses.

Fergie took out her binoculars. She could see a stretch of the airstrip from where they were.

"Let me look."

Fergie handed the glasses to the girl.

Once she'd adjusted the lenses, Cricket looked over the neighboring spread from the back of her horse. "Oh my gosh. Is that a road?"

"It's part of an airstrip," Fergie said. "A landing field."

"I *thought* I've heard planes at night before."

Al dismounted and started to tie Ol' Sal's reins to a limb.

"Just hand them to me," Cricket said.

Fergie got off Bob and stretched her back before she handed over the reins. She glanced toward the ranch where they planned to trespass. At least she couldn't see anyone moving about.

"You know who you guys are like," Cricket said, interrupting Fergie's thoughts.

"Who?"

"Those knights of old, the ones from the Round Table."

"You mean the ones who rode out to do battle while the king sat home on his... throne. Yeah, let's call it throne."

"Well, I think it's noble of you, all the same. And if it's a quest, I hope it means you bring back my dad."

"We hope so too," Fergie said. "We surely do."

Cricket watched them climb over the cattle fence. Fergie turned and gave a wave back. Then Cricket started back the way they had come, leading the two horses alongside Diablo.

There goes our escape route. Fergie shook her head. They had a long day of walking ahead. Al had started off, and she followed closely behind, glad she'd thought to switch to her lower-heeled boots for the day. They made walking across the clutter of loose rock and scattered bunches of grass easier, and they could provide a bit more speed, too, if she needed it. Before the day was over, she figured she might just have to use them in earnest.

Chapter Seventeen

A two-rut makeshift road led away from the airfield. Al and Fergie followed it, all the time keeping a careful eye out for cover. The land around them on the unworked ranch seemed stark and semi-barren. Heat radiated from the ground, while the sun cooked them from above. Having to stay aware so they would not be spotted and to keep moving long distances across the hard-packed, hot ground began to take a toll on them. Al didn't say anything because Fergie didn't, but he could see she was stopping more often to take deep breaths. He suddenly knew why the Maras he'd seen had been using gators to move across the ranch.

The stiff wind persisted but failed to cool them. The breeze felt like a harsh rasp against his skin. Fergie tugged a red bandana out of her pocket and tied it around her neck. Al nearly said something about that being an enemy gang's colors, but if they were spotted by any of the Maras, that would be the least of their worries.

Every flutter of a bouncing limb in the distance or sudden burst into flight by a bird froze them in their steps.

A couple of times, they eased off the makeshift road to crouch in the shadows of a scrap of scrub brush to drink a sip from their canteens. On one occasion, Al suggested that they might nibble at a tortilla, but Fergie just shook her head. He wasn't hungry himself but sought to fill the pensive moment with a calming activity, and putting something in their stomachs might help them if they needed the energy to cut and run.

Al looked closely at a low, shadowy overhang of loose rocks in a pile at the base of a prickly-pear cactus patch to their right. That sure looked like a fine spot for a rattler to live. When he looked back to the ruts ahead of him, he saw a rattlesnake right in front of them, coiled and ready to strike. He held out an arm to stop Fergie.

"I see it," she said. She reached to her back, and her hand came back holding her Glock.

"No," he said. "We'd better not make any noise."

She gave an exaggerated sigh and put the pistol back where she'd had it. She looked around, found a couple of loose rocks, and heaved them at the snake, not hitting it directly but stirring it up even more. A copperhead or a water moccasin would probably have come at them after that sort of agitation—they could get aggressive. But the rattler had had enough and slithered away from its sunny spot, opening the road to them again.

"We could have just gone around it," Al said.

"Where's the fun in that?" Fergie grinned at him.

At last, they crested a slope, and he could see buildings down below. He reached out to put a hand on Fergie's arm, not daring to speak. Sentries could have been anywhere with a militaristic gangbanger group like the one they faced. From what he'd seen before, he guessed they were being trained for something, and he had no intention of being part of their practice.

Al was sweating pretty freely and reached up to rub at his forehead. Fergie's skin had a moist sheen. Slowly, they hugged what scraps of cover and shadow they could find and slipped away from the ruts to ease toward the buildings through rougher unused ground.

The closer they got, the more still and deserted everything seemed.

Wind swirled in dust eddies, and an occasional dried bit of displaced brush bounced along like tumbling sagebrush, although that kind of sage wasn't native to that part of Texas.

After what seemed like an hour of careful creeping, they slipped into the shadowed side of the nearest outbuilding, a bunkhouse of sorts. Though darker in the shade, it was no cooler, and the wind seemed hotter. Al sidled along the building's outer wall until he could rise slowly and peep inside.

Nothing. Rows of cots close together lined each side, but he neither saw nor heard anyone moving about.

Fergie pressed closer to him. He shrugged and started for the door. They had to ease around a corner of the wind-scrubbed wooden building to find the entrance. As they moved toward it, Al rose to peek inside again. Nothing.

At the door, he took a deep breath, reached for the knob, and swung it open. He looked then slipped inside. Fergie had been looking all around them. She came inside a moment later.

"I don't see a soul," she whispered.

Al could see cots for at least thirty men who didn't mind being almost on top of the cot next to them. The smell in the barracks was dry but slightly pungent, with a locker-room sort of tang to it that he felt in his eyes. He smelled their stale sweat and the light oil they'd used to clean their weapons. *It must be swell living like this.* He pointed to a door at one end that didn't look like it led outside.

Making as little sound as possible, they went to it. Al opened the door and flinched when it made a rusty-sounding screech. No one was inside what looked like a bathroom big and dank enough for a group that size.

He shook his head. They went back to the door and eased outside. *Only a couple more buildings to check.* They'd certainly seen no sign of Baron or anyone else. That didn't comfort Al but instead put him more on edge.

The next building turned out to be some large sort of barn turned garage, with a place where the gators had probably sat running along one wall. A couple of the small trucks and a motorcycle, all of which he recognized, were tucked into one end.

Al went closer to a pile of wood from crates that had been opened. He kneeled and sniffed at them—Cosmoline. In one crate, he saw a couple of M-16s still in their plastic bags and gooey coatings. There were other unopened crates of grenades and a couple of crates marked MANPADS. Those were heavy stuff, the kind of shoulder-launched stinger missiles that didn't belong in civilian hands.

His picture of what was going on became clearer. Planes were rushing in this sort of stuff, which meant they had weapons trafficking—and in a hurry. The military training more than suggested someone gearing up for a serious confrontation. He looked toward Fergie.

"I know we should call this in," she said. "But knowing how the feds tromp about with something like this, any hostages might be collateral damage. First, let's find Baron if we can."

He nodded and followed her toward the door.

Not only had they not seen a single person, they had not seen any sign of where Baron might have been held.

Outside, a set of newer ruts and a few footprints the wind hadn't erased took off into a barren field broken only by a few straggling trees.

They moved on to the house, crossing a courtyard of flagstone to approach the white-stone ranchero main building. It must have been a productive ranch at some point. Al wondered for a fleeting moment how much some unnamed buyer from Mexico had paid for the whole place, almost certainly with cartel money.

The inside looked dark and empty, but Al went all the way around once. He glanced to Fergie. She was taut as an overstrung violin. She nodded and swallowed.

He reached for the back-door knob, found it unlocked, and turned it, and they entered. Without a word they went from room to room. Neither dared yell, "Clear!" but he felt it each time he found a room empty and could let out the breath he was holding.

When they at last were back in the kitchen, Al felt only partial relief. "I wonder where they are off to?"

"I'd almost rather have found them here than have to start all over," Fergie said.

Al looked around the room, opening the fridge door and then a pantry. Food, the kind that could keep but could be fixed into group meals, had been bought in great volume. Huge bags of dried beans, flour, rice, and white onions lined the bottom of the pantry below shelves of canned goods, bottles, and jars. The fridge was halfway filled with bottles of water and far too few fresh vegetables for a group of this size, unless he counted bowls of jalapenos that were just starting to get wrinkled skins. He took out a couple of bottles of water and handed one to Fergie.

She opened hers and drank half of it at a go.

"What now, chief?" Al asked.

She grinned. "I must say, you've done awfully well with me running this case so far."

"What can I say? It's your case."

"Still."

He finished off the bottle of water he had and tilted his head at her. "The chief danger in life is rigidity. You know, at our age and all. I'm trying to stay flexible."

"I'm as surprised as you are," she said.

"Yeah, I didn't think I was capable of that, but apparently I am." He tossed his empty bottle into an open trash bag that served the kitchen. "So what now?"

She stepped closer and gave him a hug.

"What was that for?"

"You know." She stepped back and looked out the kitchen's window. "I surely don't look forward to starting off on foot again, following that trail we saw lead away from here."

"I have an idea." Al waved a hand and took off, going out the door and heading for the garage.

Fergie followed along closely, still looking about all the way.

Inside, Al went over to the vehicles that remained. He grinned for the first time. "Look. Gino, that pal of ours who was on the prod, left the key in it." He pointed to the motorcycle.

He had noticed that the windshield of one of the trucks had been replaced—the machines they'd damaged had been repaired, quickly and roughly. With its scrapes, scratches, and dents, the bike looked like it had taken a tumble, but the polishing rag on it said someone was fussing over it, so it would probably run.

"Oh, Al." But Fergie stayed close as Al made sure the fuel tank was full and walked the bike outside. He climbed on.

Without a word, Fergie got on behind him. Al kick-started the machine, and it grumbled to life. He could have smiled again if they weren't headed right into the teeth of what might well have been a far stickier situation. Almost certainly, it would be, he thought.

He turned the Harley in a wide arc and took off, following the tracks of the gators and men who had been on foot. The wind pressed hard against them, almost rocking the bike a time or two. For the first time, he didn't see a trail of dust rising behind them, as the wind swept it away almost as soon as it started to rise.

Chapter Eighteen

Darren sat on one end of a worn brown couch. Dewey was tilted back in a matching but equally weathered recliner. Darren sat up, reached for the remote, and cut off the sound.

Dewey's eyes fluttered and opened. "What?"

"Did you hear something?"

"Hell no."

"Shhh." Darren tilted his head. "There. I heard something again."

He got up and went to the front window, where the curtains were pulled against the rising heat of the day. He pulled the edge of the curtain enough to look out through the crack.

At first he saw nothing, just the wide open nothing of their stupid ranch. Then he saw a bit of movement low to the ground far to his right. He scanned back to the left, more slowly and carefully. *Yep. Something or someone is out there. Several someones!*

"Hey, Dewey."

"Yeah?"

"You remember that time you woke with those stabbing chest pains, thought you were dying, and erased all the good porn stored on your computer?"

"Yeah."

"You may need to do that again." He spun and ran across the room to the wooden gun rack hanging over the fireplace mantel. He hesitated. *Shotgun or rifle?* He grabbed for the .243 Remington with a scope, which he had used when there were still deer on the spread. It was the rifle his father had passed on to him as a boy, proudly and prophetically enough calling it a "poacher's rifle." When he tugged open the wooden drawer below the guns, it came loose in his hands. A box of shotgun shells fell to the floor and broke open, the shells rolling in several directions. He grabbed the box of rifle ammo midair as it fell. He let the drawer fall to the floor in a wooden rattle.

Dewey dropped the recliner's foot lift to the floor, got to his feet, and lumbered as fast as he could to the rack. He grabbed the Wells Fargo-style shotgun, a 12-gauge double-barreled stagecoach model with an eighteen-inch barrel, good for shooting to about twenty feet away. He got to his knees and started gathering up shotgun shells and shoving them into his pockets.

Darren was halfway across the room, rushing toward the front door, when he heard a noise behind him. He spun and saw three young Latino men all with automatic rifles pointed at him. They filed in from the kitchen and fanned out across that side of the room.

"Oh shit." Dewey started to lift the shotgun.

"No. No. I'd put that down if I were you," one of the young men said with an accent but in clear and firm English.

As if to underscore his instruction, the front door swung open, and three more men burst inside, each with matching automatic guns lifted and ready.

Darren glanced toward Dewey then lowered his deer rifle to the floor and closed his eyes.

?

Mauricio entered the house when he got a wave from Isaác, who stood in the open doorway. As he went inside, he said to Isaác, "Get that and bring it inside as well." He pointed at a wooden rocking chair that sat on the far end of the porch, where it was probably out of the direct sunlight in the late afternoons.

"But it only has one arm."

"Tha's all we gonna need."

Inside, the living room seemed dimmer after being in direct sunlight. A funky dry smell of old socks and infrequent bathing permeated the air.

Two of the recruits were bringing a straight-backed chair from the kitchen. At a glance, Mauricio could tell the tall blond one was the pack leader. He pointed to the stocky short-haired brunette man. They took him over to the chair and made him sit in it. One of them took a stretch of what looked like baling twine and started to tie him in place with that.

Isaác put the rocking chair into the far corner, and two men steered the blond man toward it. Once he was seated with a gun leveled at his middle, the other recruit headed for the kitchen.

"See if you can find silver tape," Mauricio said. "These guys like that kind of thing."

When the man came out of the kitchen with a partial roll of silver duct tape, the blond guy with a ponytail made a surge to get out of the chair. Three of them wrangled him back into it, and one of them started taping his wrists in place—his right arm down to the side of the chair, his left extended out onto the remaining arm of the chair. They raised his ankles and taped them to the back of the rocker, high enough up where he couldn't use his toes to rock.

Once he was firmly in place, Mauricio stepped closer. He reached out a hand to rock the chair. "This relaxes you, no? I hear a rocking chair is good for that."

No kind of relaxation showed on the blond guy's face. Instead, his eyes were open wide.

Mauricio slowly slid the machete at his side out of its sheath. He felt the edge. "You did a good job sharpening, Isaác." He bent closer until his face was only inches away from the other man's face. "You guys like cutting off fingers, no?"

The blond guy's hand on the chair arm clenched into a fist, hiding the fingers that had been extended.

"Tha's okay with me, but you gonna lose a whole hand that way. What do they call you?"

"I'm Darren." He nodded toward the other side of the room. "That's Dewey."

"Where is the money? And where is the meth lab?"

"What?"

"You hear me."

"I don't know what you're talking about."

"Okay. Spread those fingers. The first one, she hardly hurts at all."

"Don't tell him nothin'!" Dewey yelled.

"Will you shut up?" Darren clenched his fist tighter. "There's nothing to tell."

As soon as Dewey yelled, Mauricio grinned. He turned slowly toward Dewey, and with the machete hanging at this side, he walked toward where Dewey was tied to the chair. "I think we have—what do you call it?—the weak link here."

"Mouth closed, Dewey!" Darren yelled.

Mauricio chuckled. Their yelling was like an auction from hell, one that would work in his own favor.

Dewey tried to see around Mauricio's body, which was blocking his view of Darren. But tied to a chair the way he was, all he could do was move his head like an owl.

"I mean it!" Darren yelled. "Don't you say a damned thing!"

That was about enough. Mauricio picked up the silver roll of tape and held it out to Isaác. He didn't need to explain. He could hear a strip being torn off and then only loud, desperate mumbling behind the tape from Darren's direction.

He grinned. Dewey's head was bobbing from side to side.

Mauricio lifted the machete's blade until it was inches from Dewey's nose.

"You guys like to cut people, eh?"

"No. No. No."

"Why don't I believe you? But since you say you have no meth lab, what was tha' about?"

Dewey licked his lips then closed his mouth tightly until his lips quivered and began to turn a lighter color.

Mauricio lowered the machete blade until it rested on Dewey's thigh. He slowly slid the blade across the taut blue jeans until threads split. Then the blade slid across flesh. Blood began to ooze out into the fabric.

Dewey's eyes opened wide. He stared down at his leg. "What the hell?"

"You have something you want to tell me, tha' you need to tell me."

"No, I..."

Mauricio flicked his wrist, and the blade landed with a thunk on the wood of the chair's leg. He bent to pick up a finger. He held it up in front of Dewey's face.

"Oh, holy..."

Mauricio bent to poise the machete blade for another blow.

"Wait. Wait. Wait. I'll tell you."

"I thought you would." Mauricio straightened.

"We don't have anything to do with drugs... right now. We were holding Baron to get a ransom for him."

"How much?"

"A hundred thousand."

Mauricio bent forward and extended the machete blade until its edge was poised inches from Dewey's face.

"Five hundred thousand. Five. We were going for half a million." Dewey's pitch had gone up into the realm of hysteria.

"Someone has that kind of money?"

"Yes. The woman on the ranch down the way from ours. We were about to set up the drop."

"You are sure it can work?"

"The woman, she's in on it. She set it up. We were almost there."

"Why would they pay?"

"It's her son."

"Why would she do this thing?"

"It's the only way she can get past her husband's concertina-wire prenup agreement and get her hands on any serious cash."

"She sounds kind of evil. I theenk I like her."

"You would. My hand. I can feel it bleeding."

While Isaác stepped close with a strip of silver tape and bent to apply it as a makeshift bandage, Mauricio asked, "Then you will do this?"

"It... it can't be me. Darren has to make the call. He disguises his voice."

Mauricio waved to Isaác. The two of them stepped to the door and went out into the wind.

"I theenk we see some money here after all." He rarely showed excitement, but when he was stirred up, his accent slipped a bit—no big deal when he was just speaking to the others.

Isaác nodded.

"Less get this started."

?

The phone rang. Meryl looked up at Gaby, who was coming across the living room, bringing a mug of coffee toward where she sat.

Meryl bolted up out of the chair and ran to the phone, glancing around to make sure Colin wasn't close. She snatched up the phone mid-ring. "What?"

The voice was muffled, as if someone was speaking through a towel into a bucket. But she knew who it was. "Have the money by tomorrow at nine p.m. Leave it in a black leather bag at the roadside rest twelve miles from your front gate. Will you do it?"

"Yes. Oh, yes." Meryl caught movement from the corner of her eye.

Colin came in from the kitchen and rushed across the room.

Gaby lowered the hot mug of coffee she held to the end table beside where Meryl had been sitting. She scooted across the room for the kitchen doorway as quickly as she could.

Colin snatched the phone away from Meryl's hand. "No!" he yelled into it.

An undisguised Latino voice boomed over the phone, loudly enough that Meryl could hear it clearly. "You don't pay, you get him back in pieces."

"Not gonna happen!" Colin shouted into the phone but glared at Meryl.

Who the hell was that? She grabbed for the phone, but he held it out of reach.

"The money. Must have the money ready!"

"No!" He slammed the phone back onto its holder.

"You're killing him!" Meryl shouted. "You're going to kill Baron." She had no idea who was behind the new Latino voice, but there had been real menace there. The whole thing had spun out of control. She ran from the room, holding her hands up to her face, angrier with herself than anything but unable to hold back the sobbing.

?

Mauricio handed the phone back to Darren, who hung up. He turned to Mauricio, who stood looking out the window.

"Did I hear that correctly?" Darren asked, his voice a mere squeak.

"Yes." Mauricio spun and walked away a few steps.

"They said no." Darren held the one hand that they'd freed, the hand that could have been missing some digits by then, over the closed phone. He was fixated on the guy he'd figured out was the Maras leader, who glanced back over his shoulder at him for a moment.

Mauricio turned to Darren and Dewey. "Thees is not good news for you, no?" He waved for the men waiting with machetes. They stepped forward with an undisguised eagerness in their eyes.

Darren and Dewey both began to scream as loudly as they could.

Mauricio went to the door and opened it. He stood just outside the room. There would be splatter. He could always count on some splatter at such moments.

Chapter Nineteen

Escovar wove his swaying way through the center aisle of the moving bus, stepping around stretched legs. At the back, he opened a cooler and took out a plastic bag of home-style tortillas. He took one out and held it in one hand while he added a single slice of bologna. Then, using a plastic fork, he added diced white onion and sliced pieces of pickled jalapeno. He rolled it into a wrap then flipped open another cooler and looked through the offerings of long-neck Coronas and cans of Tecate and Bud Light. He reached for a bottle of water. Maybe he'd have a beer or two after.

He started back up through the bus to his seat. Most of the seats in the bus were filled, and the men all jostled around in a festive mood.

Almost every one of them had one or two pistols, a knife or two, and a long automatic. But what made Escovar grin were the two cases in the back of the bus, holding the four shoulder-fired missile launchers that could work ground to air or ground to ground. They were going to make very large booms. That was always fun.

His seat was all the way in the front, behind the driver. Members of Puro Tango Blast had no hierarchy or chain of command like so many of the other cartel-fueled gangs did. He sat down beside Pablo. "You hear anything more from your brother Roberto?"

Pablo shook his head. He was the one with the coordinates on his cell phone, and they were getting close. "Just the one time, but we know where to go now. It changed a little. I let the other bus know."

Escovar glanced toward the window. He couldn't see out because they'd covered the windows with makeshift banners, all proclaiming the Houston Astros the kings of the world. His pal Estaban had thought of that—it was supposed to make the yellow ISD school bus look like it was hauling kids on a field trip. The other bus coming from the other direction was marked in the same way. The buses were Jorge's idea. He had known Jorge since they were at Huntsville together. They had talked about caravans of vehicles. Jorge had said that would be too conspicuous, and he knew someone at the repair garage where they kept backup school buses, each able to hold seventy-two passengers.

The only time they had stopped for fuel, some young gringo had sneaked up and used a marker to write: "Go Astros... And Take the Rockets with you!" Any other time, they would have gone out after that punk kid, but they had stayed inside the bus.

Neither bus was full to capacity, but they had brought 114 members along for the outing, all promised a chance for a go at some Maras. He knew they had them outnumbered almost three to one. The men behind Escovar were laughing and rollicking as if they *were* on a field trip. None of them had gotten into the beer yet, but they were having fun. He smiled. As far as he was concerned, it was going to be little more than just a festive outing, although one with a little shooting and maybe some cutting.

?

Al was watching the rutted trail for dips and holes and looked up in time to see a cabin in the distance. He killed the motorcycle engine at once, and Fergie hopped off. He eased the bike over to a stretch of tall prairie grass and laid it down on its side, still warm. He waited a few ticks to make sure the grass didn't catch fire. Then he and Fergie started off, hiking toward the cabin.

"If you were the sheriff, what would you be doing?" she asked.

"I'd have tapped Meryl and Colin's phone lines and waited for the call." He held up a hand. No more talking. They were getting too close. He watched for any sign of movement near the cabin.

Each step made the dry grass crackle like Rice Krispies. He winced at every sound.

The closer they got to the cabin, the more carefully he looked around. He could see no one in any direction. That was good.

Around the front of the cabin, packed gravel marked where a vehicle could park. Tire tracks led away, but no vehicle was around. He and Fergie scouted all the way around the cabin once before moving nearer.

Al slid close to the outside wall and eased up to peek inside through a window. He saw a figure sitting in a chair. He nodded to Fergie. "See what you can see."

She popped up, looked inside, then lowered herself back down. "Just one person in there. It could be Baron. We saw pictures of him at the house."

"Looks like he's all alone in there. Let's go take a closer look."

When they got to the front door, they positioned themselves on either side of it. Al reached to turn the doorknob and opened the door. He rushed inside, Fergie right behind him. They pointed their guns in opposite directions, sweeping every corner of the small interior.

"Clear," Fergie said.

Al gave the room one more look and hurried over to Baron, more sure it was him. On the way, he swept a paring knife off the kitchen counter. Carrying it, he moved close and cut the tape at Baron's ankles then at his wrists. He'd seen the finger in the mailer envelope, so he wasn't surprised to see the gauze and tape wrapping on Baron's left hand.

The moment Al stripped the silver tape away from Baron's mouth, he said, "Behind you."

Al spun.

Two young Maras stood in the doorway, both pointing M-16s at Fergie and him. "The guns and cell phones. Put them on the floor."

Al looked toward Fergie then back at the two men. All the calculations he could do in his head said they didn't have a chance. But would the men just kill them anyway? Well, they hadn't killed Baron. Maybe...

"Now!"

Al shrugged. He took out his pistol and cell phone and put them on the floor. Fergie did the same.

"Miguel," one of them said.

The nearest of them scurried forward. He kicked the pistols back toward the other one and scooped up the cell phones. He carried them outside. *Bam, bam!* He figured that was it for their phones.

They were in the room with just one of them, and Al thought it could be their only chance. He poised to make a leap, pretty sure he probably wouldn't make it across the room in time. But perhaps Fergie would have time to get one of the guns and defend herself. He had to take the chance.

Just before he leaped, he heard a sound and turned to see the blur of Baron surging from where he'd sat to charge directly toward the younger man with the automatic gun.

The young Salvadoran swung his rifle toward Baron.

That was all the distraction Al needed. He was across the room and kicking the gun out of the man's hands before he could fire. Maybe the kid had the safety on or was just slow with his response—Al didn't get long to ponder that. Fergie bowled the fellow down and pinned him to the floor with Baron piling on as well.

Al grabbed the falling rifle in midair and spun as Miguel rushed back inside. Al held the rifle by its barrel and swung, the stock slamming into Miguel's stomach. He dropped his rifle and slumped to the floor with a grunt.

Al picked up the other rifle. He made sure the safeties were off and pointed the guns at Miguel. His eyes were watering, and he didn't look ready to rise again soon.

"Just a sec." Baron stood quickly while Fergie held the other downed Salvadoran in a half-nelson. Baron came rushing back in with a handful of lengths of baling twine. He helped Fergie get the guy she held into the chair where Baron had been tied. In moments, they had him tied tightly. Baron placed a bit of the duct tape that had held him across the guy's mouth.

The moment they turned to deal with Miguel, he got a whole new surge of energy. He must have felt some of the same desperation Al had felt earlier. His eyes opened widely, and he leaped to his feet in desperation, charging not for the door but right at them.

Al let the automatic rifles he held drop to the floor. As soon as Miguel got within a step of him, Al moved forward and, using Miguel's energy against him, flipped him in the air and landed him onto his back with a hard *umph* onto the wooden floor. He held Miguel down with one foot on his chest while Baron and Fergie rushed in to hogtie him.

Baron pulled another matching chair over from the table for Miguel. He and Fergie lifted him onto it, tied him to it, and gagged him the same way as he did the other Salvadoran.

Baron was still huffing and puffing. "It's sure going to feel good to get out of here." He nodded toward the tied men. "What about these guys?"

"We'll leave them here," Fergie said. "Someone knows they're here and will come back for them."

?

Wes had been watching Cricket since she rode back all in a lather from who knew where. She seemed restless and twitchy, more so than usual, and had been pacing back and forth in a pensive way. She had even left Diablo saddled in the corral as if she seemed undecided about something.

Suddenly, she made up her mind. She ran to Diablo, led him out of the corral, hopped on, and was off in a dusty cloud of a streak.

"Bo!" he yelled. "You'd best come. Miss Cricket may be headed for some kind of trouble, I fear, and we'd best follow."

Bo didn't say a thing as he lumbered out of the back. He motioned for Ike the dog to stay and was already saddling a horse by the time Wes turned to him. Wes rushed to grab a saddle himself.

The two of them rode out across the pasture, being more careful than fast. There was no way their horses could keep up with Diablo.

At the gate on the far corner of the spread, they followed her tracks, opening and closing the gate behind them.

"That girl takes after her grandmother sometimes," Wes said, "and that's not altogether a good thing."

They came at last to where Diablo was tied to a scrub brush, already munching on the grass he could reach.

Wes and Bo hopped off their horses, tied them next to Diablo, and followed the footprints. They climbed over the cattle fence where she had. The trail Al, Fergie, and Cricket had made wasn't hard to follow, but Wes slowed when he could see buildings ahead. He hesitated, looking about carefully. He and Bo could be headed into danger if people were present. He was glad he had waited when he saw a tiny figure leaving the group of buildings and heading off in another direction. Cricket had already looked around and was moving on. Wes and Bo walked as fast as they could toward her.

"Wait! Cricket! Hold up, there!" he yelled.

But the blasted girl just moved faster, tired as she must be—even he and Bo were breathing harder after their hike.

Wes broke into a run and tried to cut off some ground, with Bo struggling to keep up. Cricket began to run too. She was young and so much faster.

After a while, the two men slowed to plodding steps.

"That little sprat is gonna wear our boot heels off," Wes muttered. The spread seemed to go on and on until he could finally see the deer fence ahead. The gate was open, a clipped rusty chain lying in a pile on the ground. They passed through the gate onto the even rougher going of Darren and Dewey's spread. He couldn't see Cricket, but her footsteps seemed to waver, and he thought she might be slowing.

For what seemed another mile, they hiked up and down the swells of browning grass, amid clumps of cacti and loose rocks.

At last, they strode over a rise, and Wes could see her, sitting down on an ottoman-sized rock for a moment, resting. She started to rise. He could see a cabin in the near distance.

"Wait. Don't run. We'll go with you. We're close enough and too far away to go back just yet. Let us walk a spell with you."

Whether she was tuckered or agreed that they might as well be together to approach the cabin, she waited.

Wes looked back. His feet and back hurt, but he kept moving. Bo was in no better shape. A sheen of sweat covered his face, and he mopped at it with his handkerchief, but he never said a word of complaint. They moved as quickly as they could up to where the girl waited on them.

?

Al picked up the Salvadorans' automatic rifles, and Fergie was halfway to the door when it burst open so firmly it slapped with a wooden thud against the wall.

Al went into a crouch with both weapons pointed toward the door.

"Daddy!" Cricket stood in the doorway. She ran across the room to throw herself into Baron's open arms.

Al lowered the rifles.

"You shouldn't be out here, honey," Fergie said.

"Don't worry. I brought troops."

Two men stepped up to the doorway so those inside could see them.

As he blinked against the brighter light outside, it took Al a moment to recognize Wes and the towering Bo.

"They came along to protect me," she said.

"They should have stopped you from coming," Fergie said.

"Lord knows that was our intention. You don't know Missy Cricket here if you think we could have stopped her," Wes said. "We chased her all the way here, trying to get her to stay at home. But I expect she would have come on her own, anyway. This way, we can make sure she makes it back home okay."

"I'd rather she hadn't come out here at all," Fergie said, "but I'm glad you followed her."

"And I may seem to be on step fourteen of a twelve-step program," Wes said, "but I was a marine once."

"I'm surprised she didn't bring Colin," Al whispered to Fergie.

"He maybe hasn't decided which side he's on," Fergie whispered back.

Cricket was looking Baron over, taking in the scrapes and bruises. "Who did this to you, Daddy?"

"Darren and Dewey tied me up." He might have said more about them cutting off his finger. Cricket was staring at his hand.

"Did you hurt yourself?"

"A little. But it'll be okay when we all go home."

"I thought Darren and Dewey were your friends." She looked up at him.

"Let's just say they're not getting a Christmas card this year."

?

"Have you seen Colin?" Meryl asked Gaby.

The cook was bent over a *molcajete*, a large basalt mortar. She was pounding with a matching stone pestle at some *epazote* leaves and dried chili peppers to make a sauce for dinner. She looked up and shrugged.

Meryl went out the back kitchen door onto the patio. She saw Colin come out of the stable and head toward the house. He was taking long, brisk strides. His head was down, and he seemed deep in thought.

She took off at a near run. "Colin. Colin!"

He stopped walking and looked up.

"What are you doing?" she asked.

"Trying to find out where the hell everyone is around here. I can't find a soul, and..."

"Colin. We need to talk."

He frowned and looked away for a moment. The frown was still there when he turned back to her. He shook his head. "I think we already understand each other."

He pushed around her and continued toward the house.

She turned slowly to watch him. Her insides felt like that point when making coffee in which the water first begins to send up bubbles, slowly at first, then more quickly. She felt just about to boil, and he was the one headed for the scalding.

Whatever was going to happen had to happen quickly. She couldn't imagine that Baron had very much time left at all, and if something happened to him, she was going to have to face being responsible for that the rest of her life. She tried hard to imagine how that Latino voice on the phone fitted in with what she, Darren, and Dewey had discussed. But they had leaped the rails from that when they'd asked for five hundred thousand instead of a hundred. She would very much like to lay hands on them, but that would have to wait. Colin, however, was within her reach and her power to do whatever was needed.

Chapter Twenty

Escovar's bus pulled over at a rest stop marked as a picnic stop, meaning there were no bathrooms. But any of the men who needed a restroom could slip over to the three-strand barbed wire fence and watch for a break in the passing traffic. The men were still festive but slightly more subdued.

His phone rang. When he answered, all he heard was "We're here."

He nodded at the bus driver, and the last couple of Tango Blast members still outside came scrambling for the bus's open door.

The two yellow buses rolled to the front of Darren and Dewey's ranch from two directions. They turned in, one after the other, and paused long enough to send scouts ahead on foot.

The buses moved slowly. Within moments, the scouts came back and waved. Both buses stopped where they were, and the men poured out.

Escovar saw José running along with the scouts. They held him by the arms. Escovar waved them off. "He's my son."

As they came up to the lead bus, José ran to his father and grabbed him in a hug.

"Hey, bambino. Why are you crying?"

"It's Roberto. He got caught stealing... and... and..."

Escovar squeezed José closer. "You don't have to say nothin' else."

Pablo pressed closer to hug his brother while Escovar went back inside the bus. He went back to the boxes and stood there, looking down at the boxes stamped in black ink: MANPADS. It stood for man-portable air-defense systems. But he knew he could use them for ground targets as well. For a moment, he was back at the baptismal font, and Roberto, his firstborn, was being christened. Rosalinda had said Roberto meant "bright and shining." The baby had beamed up at them.

Rosalinda had died just after Escovar got out. It was as if she had used herself up taking care of the boys until he was released. And now Roberto was dead, at the hands of those pig Maras. With Rosalinda no longer on earth, it was up to him to do something about José.

His hands clenched into fists. He took long, deep breaths. The stinger missiles could be like lightning bolts. They were by no means cheap, but if they took out the likes of the Maras and especially their leader, that would be money well spent. He opened a box and took out the last one of the shoulder-held missile launchers.

When he went back out to join the others, he had its strap over his shoulder. He also carried two AK-47s. He held one out to José. He also handed José an oversized plain black T-shirt. "Slip this on. At least you can cover up those Salvadoran colors. That way, you won't get shot by one of ours."

José pulled on the shirt. It hung loosely like a skirt. He checked the weapon his father had given him and nodded. Escovar smiled at the businesslike way José had gone locked and loaded.

"Now, let's go do something in your brother's memory," Escovar said. "We'll pay these Maras a visit."

In prison, being a Puro Tango Blast member meant protection against the other gangs, the Aryans, the Mexikanemi, and the Texas Syndicate. Out in the post-prison world, being a member was about money, fighting, and power. He'd gotten his three sons in without a Cora Check, which would have meant they had to fight at least two other established members. Boys that age were needed to infiltrate the Maras, the Salvadorans, a gang that hoped to claw its way into space the Tangoes occupied, and now he had lost Roberto to these savages.

No one had ordered the Tangoes to be at the confrontation with the Maras. The Maras had invited them, and the Tangoes showed up in numbers, the way people would join together to combat a swarm of cockroaches. They all wore eager faces, with their eyes glittering and their teeth clenched tightly, checking their weapons and falling into fluid formations to move forward.

Since Tango Blast members didn't have the hierarchy of rank the way some other prison-spawned gangs did, they approached the situation with experience and practicality, spreading into two large enveloping wings that moved toward the farmhouse. Escovar worked his way to the extreme tip of the right wing, eager for the first clash of battle. It wasn't a city drive-by—he hoped it was going to be smash-up, in-your-face rumbling.

?

Inside the house, Mauricio looked around at the open drawers dropped to the floor and piles of stuff from the closets. They'd searched Darren and Dewey's place from one end to the other, including the men's wallets, and had gotten only a little over three hundred dollars.

He shook his head at the two men still in their chairs, their heads resting in their laps. Isaác had done that. He was creative that way. *The boy probably should be in art school somewhere.* That made Mauricio chuckle—as if someone like Isaác could give up the banger's life.

Darren's eyes were open and staring, fixed, a little surprised, really. The dark-haired one's head seemed almost peaceful.

"Hey. Come here and take a look." Isaác pulled the closed front curtain to one side. He pointed out across the dead or dying grass of what had been a pasture.

Even from where he stood, it looked to Mauricio as though men were starting to appear over the tall grass, a lot of them, and they were coming this way.

In their digging through the household goods, Mauricio had come across a pair of field glasses. He rushed over to the kitchen counter, where he'd seen them last. He scooped them up and headed back to the window. As he got them into focus, he snapped, "Get the men. Every one of them."

The approaching men were coming in two waves, one from the left and the other from the right.

"Tangoes," he said. He scanned the approaching lines of them. There were easily twice as many men as he had, and his were still pretty green. As a leader, Mauricio prided himself on doing well with what he had. Normally, being the underdog, he would have gone for the leader of the opposition and cut his legs out from under him. But the damned Tangoes had no clear leader. If he took one out, another would rise in his place. It was like fighting a many-headed hydra.

He thought on it. The hole in the middle was the weakness. They'd stretched their flanking wings too wide. If he could get men through that hole and come around from the back, he'd have them all.

"We need to break them up, get in behind them," he said to Isaác.

"I'll be leading them astray by retreating with most of the men. You, Isaác, will charge up the middle, get in behind them, and tear them up from behind as only you can."

"These men are on foot. I could take the truck they had, charge through the hole, and do what you want."

"*Bueno.* Do it. Take a third of the men. Call me when you are behind them, ready to attack."

"And you?"

"I will lead the rest back toward where we came in, for now. When you call, I'll swing back and attack their nearest flank. Now go. *Pronto!*" Even as he said it, Mauricio mentally gave Isaác a less-than-even chance. But that Salvadoran was a banger, and he would have fun. It would be one big drive-by to him. Mauricio chuckled to himself.

He kept the binoculars, slipping the strap over his head to let the field glasses hang.

Mauricio moved as fast as he was able. He waved to the others to follow him to the gators. He had taken a bullet to the knee once long ago and had lost the speed of youth. But the recruits were in place and armed, and as soon as he plopped into the lead gator, the caravan took off.

He glanced back. Isaác already had the truck heading directly at the open center of the Tango Blast group, at the gap between the two approaching lines. One man hung outside the passenger-seat window with an M-16, and the back of the truck bristled with rifle barrels.

As soon as they were in range, the crackle of rifle fire broke out in bursts and strings, with shots coming from the Maras in the truck as well as from the Tangos nearest the center.

He willed the gator to go faster, but a gator is capable only of ponderous movement over ground as rough as the untended pastures had become.

?

Escovar grinned when he saw the reddish-brown truck barreling and bouncing along toward the center of their lines. He knew what awaited the vehicle ahead. One third of the Tango force was in each flanking wing. The hole in the center was on purpose. The other third of the Tango Blast members waited to ambush the incoming gang in a line out of sight and to the rear.

Even though the back of the truck was packed with men shooting their rifles, the truck first had to run the gauntlet of men shooting at them from the inside tips of the front wings. Then they would run into the full force of those waiting. He had hoped the whole force of Maras would have come at them this way, but a good portion of the other gang was retreating as fast as they could go. The ones running were nearly outstripping those in the lumbering green gators.

?

From the passenger seat window, Isaác fired away, holding the M-16 with one hand while reaching for another clip from his bag with the other. He was enjoying the drive-by shooting of a lifetime. Shots from both sides of the Tango force were slamming into the truck, and a few men tumbled from the back, but he figured they would make it. Those damned Tangoes were shooting for the tires too. If those went, they were going to have a scramble out of the way on their hands.

"Faster!" he yelled, slammed the fresh clip into place, and fired away at the nearest Tangoes he could see. They left the ruts of the lane that led to the house and stayed aimed at the opening of men, a path that took them across a rough open pasture full of holes and small rises and drops.

The way the truck was bouncing up and down made it hard to aim, but the charm of an automatic weapon was that he could spray across the men he could see. He saw one or two go down but also heard cries from the recruits in the bed of the truck, and at least two more tumbled out onto the ground. One just lay there. The other seemed to be scrambling on hands and knees after the speeding truck, but he was soon out of sight.

They passed the ends of the flanking lines and got behind them—it was time to loop back and hit these Tangos from behind. Fewer shots from the two flanks were hitting the truck now. The half dozen recruits still in the back were firing away and taking their toll.

He turned to look ahead in time to see a fresh new line of Tangoes rise up and begin firing away at the truck. He knew at once that he'd rolled right into an ambush.

Half a dozen shots from the line ahead took out the truck's front tires even as Isaác's driver was trying to turn.

The front of the truck plowed down into the ground, digging its own ditch. The front bumper slammed into hard-packed dirt, and the truck twisted, beginning to roll onto its side.

The men in back dove off in all directions, the unfortunate ones in the direction the truck was rolling.

Isaác tucked his rifle and arms inside the cab just as it rolled right. He saw the brown dirt go by in the first roll but was too busy being tossed about inside the cab to see more as the truck rolled two more times.

He shook his head and blinked. He'd been slammed forward into the dash. Blood ran from his forehead in a trickle. He reached up to it with his right hand and found that the hand didn't work. The fingers and the hand were there but so horribly sprained that he didn't dare try picking up a pencil, much less the M-16 that lay on the floor.

He reached for a clip that had fallen from his pocket, cursing himself again when his right hand didn't work. He switched to his left hand and shoved the loose clip back into his pocket.

His driver was crumpled forward onto the steering wheel. He'd bounced into the windshield at some point in the crash. The windshield was shattered, and bits of broken glass glittered in the man's forehead, but they weren't bleeding. Isaác knew what that meant.

Bullets were slamming into the sides of the truck with loud pings.

He tried to open his door with his left hand but found it jammed. The way was blocked to his other side, which left the jagged-edged open mouth of glass that had been the windshield. He forced himself to his knees and began to squeeze out through the opening.

Bullets ricocheted off the metal hood, knocking flecks of paint up into his face.

He looked around for the others. One or two Maras were on the ground, firing back at the advancing line of those damned Tangoes.

The other spots of color around and behind the truck, Salvadoran men either shot or slammed into the hard soil when the truck wrecked, lay still.

The approaching line of men grew closer. Still hanging halfway out the window, he reached back inside and on his third try grabbed enough of the M-16 to lift it and point it with his left hand. He could barely manage to pop in a new clip. He held it as best he could and fired it at the enemy until he heard the hard click that told him to put in a new clip.

He was fumbling in his pocket with his left hand, the rifle lying on its side on the truck's hood, when he looked up and saw half a dozen men on each side, walking deliberately toward the truck. None of his men were firing. He had just a second or two to wonder how that Indian-fighter fellow Custer felt when he'd faced all those Sioux.

Rifles opened fire from what seemed like all directions and just a few paces away. He felt bullets thumping into him for a moment and could even sense his body jerking with each hit. Then he felt nothing, and everything went black.

?

Escovar shrugged as the truck barreled through their lines just as they had planned, except they had hoped to lure the whole group into the trap. They hadn't counted on the large number of them turning tail and running from an encounter, although that was exactly what it looked like was going on.

The remaining Maras, who usually enjoyed such a fierce reputation as fighters, were rushing off to the right, with a row of green gators beginning to outstrip the other Salvadorans, who were moving at a near run.

Escovar turned to José. "I thought they would stand and fight."

"That Mauricio knows he's outnumbered," José said, "but if he manages to get back to the ranch house..."

"He has more weapons there?"

"Many," José said.

Escovar would see about that. He lifted the missile launcher, prepped it, and raised it to his shoulder. He took aim at the lead gator and clicked the trigger, and it was off in a whoosh. "This one is for Roberto," he muttered.

The missile arced only lightly, whirring and twisting, leaving a trail of smoke behind, until it came down smack on the second gator in the parade. The gator blew up in a shower of green parts, shattered men, and rifles. *Ah, well. Close enough.*

His line moved faster, rushing to catch up to the fleeing Maras. The line to his left and behind, which seemed to be done with their business, collapsed into one big mass, and they ran on foot as fast as they could go.

?

When the missile hit, it rocked the gator Mauricio was in to one side, almost upsetting it. The driver righted the vehicle and kept it scrambling as fast as it could go. "*Más rápido!*" Mauricio yelled.

The driver gave him a sideways glance with a frown.

Mauricio looked back and saw some of his men scattered on the ground as if a grenade had gone off. The remaining gators were going out and around the crater and the shattered bits of the one that had been hit.

Farther back, those damned Tangoes formed a big lump of angry men that looked like hornets pouring out of a nest. They had far more men and were almost certainly better trained. The missile had scared him horribly, and he was a very hard man to scare.

"Faster!" he yelled.

The driver didn't even look at him.

As they followed the path they had used to come onto the spread, the cabin loomed into sight. Mauricio waved to a couple of the men, Gino and Angel, in the back of the gator. "Go get those two at the cabin." He thought for a moment. The man they'd left tied to a chair there would be useless as a hostage. "Finish the guy they are watching."

Gino checked his M-16, found it empty, felt in his pockets, and found no more clips. So he dropped the rifle into the gator's bed and grabbed the short double-barreled shotgun. He and Angel scrambled over the side of the moving gator and took off at a run for the cabin.

Mauricio kept his eyes on the way ahead, except for an occasional glance back, where many of his men on foot were falling far behind the gators and were breaking into a dead run, showing little discipline or

organization at all. He would have a talk with them when it was over...
if they made it. He was beginning to be less and less sure about that.

Chapter Twenty-One

"We've got to get moving," Al said. He was worried for all of them, but most of all for Cricket, whom he would just as soon not expose to more than she'd already seen.

She stood looking at the two men tied to chairs. "Are these men part of who kidnapped and hurt you?" she asked Baron.

"No. That was all Darren and Dewey, like I said, who I thought were my friends."

"I can't believe that they really did that to you." Her eyes opened wider. "Why?"

Baron looked down for a moment, probably not sure how to answer her.

"It's okay if it was, Dad. We're over it now. You're free, and Colin didn't have to pay anything. He and Auntie Gran were scrapping over that."

"I'm sorry to hear that."

"Don't worry," Cricket said. "They're scrapping most of the time, anyway. If it wasn't about you, it'd be about something else."

Baron turned to Fergie. "I owe you a lot. I was afraid I was never going to get out of this."

"You're not all the way out of this yet. Al's right. We'd better get a wiggle on."

Cricket chuckled. She could still find humor in the situation but probably because she couldn't begin to understand how dangerous a mess they were in.

Wes and Bo picked up the M-16s the two men on the chairs had carried and took the packs that held more ammunition.

Al tugged his Sig Sauer out from where he'd tucked it at the small of his back, and Fergie held her Glock.

Fergie eased closer to Al and spoke quietly. "Our number-one job now is to keep Cricket safe."

He nodded.

Wes and Bo were the first to step out the cabin door. They came rushing back in. "Get down! Get low, right away!" Wes yelled.

Fergie swept Cricket to the floor and covered her.

Baron stood staring, so Al yanked him down to the floor as well and held him there.

?

Gino and Angel were running across the open field toward the cabin when Gino caught a glimmer of red and silver hiding amid the swaying tall brown grass. "No. It can't be."

He slowed and moved closer, not believing his eyes. As soon as he was close enough to bend over and take a good look, he told Angel, "I don' know how it got here, but this is sure 'nough my bike. Look at the scratches. I was just rubbing at those."

Angel nodded. "That's your bike, all right." He looked up as if the motorcycle had fallen from the sky.

They weren't that far from the cabin. Gino could see it a short ways ahead from where the bike lay.

"Somebody rode it here. Tha's for sure," Gino said. He lifted the bike and climbed onto it, slipping the shotgun under one thigh. "Hop on."

Angel climbed on behind him, and Gino fired up the motorcycle and began moving across the former pasture, slowly at first. The ground was hard and hardly suited for speed, but it was far better than walking.

Gino opened up the motorcycle, and with the shotgun under his leg on the motorcycle seat, he wove through some of the running men who followed along behind the gators, which could go up to sixty miles per hour on a flat road. They hadn't been approaching that speed with so many men piled on, but they had to be going forty-five or so over bumpy ground.

He looked ahead toward the cabin and saw two men come out the front of it. Gringos. They sure weren't Maras.

He slowed.

"What the hell?" Angel leaned out around him to stare at the cabin.

Gino stopped the bike, sliding into a skid. "They have our guys in there. Someone's got them." It was the only way he could figure the presence of other men.

"Shoot!" he yelled at Angel, who opened up at the cabin with his M-16.

Several other straggling Maras on both sides of the cabin turned and opened fire as well.

?

Al was breathing hard even before the shots burst out and a line of holes swept across the cabin, making a waist-high line. That was an automatic weapon, for sure. Then shots began to crisscross the cabin, as if someone was trying to cover every bit of space. The shooting increased as more of the Maras seemed to join in with their rifles.

At a brief pause, probably for them to shove in new clips, Al stood long enough to knock the fridge over on its side. Unopened bottles of water spilled out as it fell, and Al kicked them aside. Fergie clutched Cricket close and moved her over to tuck her as near as she could to the fridge on the other side of the rifle fire coming at them.

The shooting started again. Wooden chips flew off the wall.

Al looked toward the men tied to the chairs and watched them jerk as bullets ripped through them. Fergie was shielding Cricket from seeing that. They wanted to prevent her from seeing any more than she had to, but he knew they would have their hands full just getting her the hell out alive.

Crouched as low as he could get, Al saw Bo slither to the door like some giant articulated python. He cracked it open, ignoring the bullets slamming into it, and was soon outside with the door closed behind him.

"Where the hell is he going?" Al asked Wes.

"Don't worry. He's not abandoning the ship." Wes checked the rifle he held and rose to fire a burst of shots back at those outside.

He was certainly a different Wes than Al had first encountered at Meryl's ranch. He was more like the men Al had stood side by side with during the military service he thought he'd left far behind.

In what seemed like only a few seconds, the door opened a crack, and Bo slithered back in, despite heavy fire. He held up two more M-16s and ammo packs.

"How...?" Fergie started to ask.

"Best not to know," Wes said. He glanced toward Cricket, who peeked out from under Fergie's protective arms.

?

Shots were returned from inside the cabin, peppering the area where Gino and the others were closing in. Men dove to the ground, shooting back, except Angel. He crumpled forward and dropped his rifle.

Gino screamed as loudly as he could and rushed to his fallen comrade. He grabbed the rifle and began firing away with it fully automatic until it was empty. He dug into Angel's pack and pulled out two more clips, shoved one of them into the rifle, and continued to fire at the cabin.

As he shot away, he saw that some of the Salvadoran men who had been flattened were getting up and starting to move again, staying low and heading off to the right, toward the ranch where they had been training.

He looked left and realized why. Those damned Tangoes were almost up to them and were moving fast.

"Damn!" He stayed to finish the next clip as well. He reached to touch the rifle's barrel and yanked his finger away. Hot. Far too warm to carry on his back. He dropped the rifle to the ground and ran to his motorcycle.

He tucked the shotgun under his leg again, fired up the motorcycle, and was off in a spray of dirt and dust.

Steady shooting sounded behind him. He glanced back. Whoever was in that cabin was still shooting away in defense, but they were taking on Tango Blast members instead of Maras. *Good.* Gino opened the motorcycle up, sped past the straggling men, and was soon able to go past the gators. They were still going flat-out but weren't going to win any NASCAR events. Nor would they beat Gino.

As he went past the lead gator, Mauricio waved him on, probably glad someone would be able to scout the way ahead and make sure their ranchero, where there were more weapons, was safe for them.

With no reason to look back, Gino lowered his head and went as fast as the path allowed.

The trail the gators had made across the open, rough fields was far from perfect, so he had to slow often and pick his way with care so he wouldn't hit a hole and end up flying over the handlebars.

He saw a clear open stretch ahead where he could open the bike up again. Even with the slow-and-go speeds, he was making far better time than Mauricio and the rest of the Maras.

Soon, he was through the opening in the deer fence and rolling along on land they had traversed often in their training as recruits, where he could really push the motorcycle and fly.

Already, he was thinking of rearming from the stores of weapons and ammo there and heading back to the fray. On the bike, he could zip around the outskirts of those damned Tangoes and pick them off with impunity. That would be the greatest drive-by ever.

He was nearly to the cluster of buildings when he saw the first black vehicles with bold letters that said ATF. Others said ICE.

No, it wasn't safe there. He slowed the bike enough to make a turn, hoping he was far enough away that they couldn't see him clearly.

His tires spun then caught, and he was off in a boil of reddish dust spraying up behind him. He would have to see if it was any safer at the next ranch. He didn't think for a moment to go back and let Mauricio know that ATF vehicles were swarming all over this place. He would figure it out.

?

Fergie held Cricket close and expected her to be crying from all the bullets sailing over their heads, thudding into the other side of the fridge, smashing objects, and breaking windows. But the little girl instead bristled with energy to defend. She lay close to the floor but cheered on the others from Meryl's ranch. "Get 'em, Wes and Bo!"

Al and Baron each rose to take quick turns firing out their windows as the four of them covered the approach to the cabin in all directions.

Cricket turned to Fergie. "You said you would find my father, and you did."

"I thought someone close was responsible. But I had no way of knowing about all this." Fergie gave a short wave at the bullets smashing into the cabin from all sides.

At a brief lull in the rain of bullets, probably those outside reloading again, Wes popped up and peeked out the gaping hole of what had been a window. He shook his head. While he was up, he slipped over to the bed and yanked the sheets off it. He went over to the two men still in chairs but no longer posing any kind of threat. He spread a sheet over each of them. When Fergie gave him a wrinkled-eyebrow look, he nodded toward the little girl. He was protecting her from the sight.

He dove back to the floor as shooting started up again.

Fergie realized in a rush what a tight family they all must have been before the craziness descended on the ranch where Baron, Cricket, Gaby, Wes, and Bo had lived. They had been a happy group of people who didn't deserve what was happening.

She looked around the cabin. "Where's Bo this time?" she asked over the rattle of bullets chewing at wood and glass.

"He'll be back," Wes said. He was busy putting another clip into the rifle he held.

Fergie wondered for a moment how low on ammo they were getting. If they ran out, they couldn't last long with a horde like the one they faced surrounding the cabin.

The door opened, and Bo once more slithered back inside, big as he was. He carried three ammo packs.

"Where'd he get those?" Fergie asked.

"Let's just say he found them," Wes said. Again, he gave a conspiratorial nod toward Cricket.

Al reached toward the ammo packs and dug through them until he said, "Ah."

He took out a small box of 9mm ammo that matched his and Fergie's guns. Since he had no spare clips, he popped his out and shoved shells into it. He took a few more bullets and put them in one pocket. He slid the box across the debris-cluttered floor to Fergie, who began to reload as well.

Wes was tying his bandana around his upper arm. Even as he did, blood began to seep through it.

"You're hurt. Here, let me help," Fergie said.

"I'm nowhere near as bad off as Bo," Wes said. "You might see to him if you have the inclination to tend to someone."

She looked over to see Bo holding a torn piece of cloth from his own shirt against a bleeding spot on his left shoulder.

"Oh my heavens." Fergie slid over closer to the big man, stripping a pillowcase off a pillow as she did.

"I want to help," Cricket said.

"Just stay put so you don't get hit."

But Cricket ignored her. She moved to the other side, at least crouching as low as she could, as Fergie used a steak knife that had fallen on the floor to cut away part of Bo's shirt. His big, hairy shoulder was bleeding from two holes.

"Looks like they're through-and-through," Fergie said. "Does it hurt?"

Bo shrugged but winced. He probably didn't want to show pain in front of Cricket.

Cricket got busy tearing the pillowcase into strips. "There's nothing wrong with being a nurse," she said, "but I want to be a doctor when I grow up. Maybe a vet."

"Just stay low," Fergie said. She could have added that Cricket's future plans might depend on that, but she was trying hard not to underscore the stark danger they faced.

She used plain water from one of the bottles that had fallen out of the fridge to clean Bo's wounds, which began to ooze as soon as she'd swept a wet cloth over the spots. She made a couple of gauze-like pads from the cloth and tied the other strips together so she could bind them around the shoulder, pressing the pads tightly against the wounds. Cricket helped as best she could, she and Fergie both staying low since bullets still pounded the cabin and shattered glass and objects inside.

"Can you move the shoulder?"

Bo tried and nodded.

"Good."

As soon as she was done, he reached to pat Cricket on the head in thanks. He looked at Fergie, perhaps struggling with how to express appreciation without hugging or touching her. The notion confused and embarrassed him, so he picked up his rifle and went back to one of the windows to stay low under it until they could hear a break in the shooting.

Al took a couple of spare clips and went to the shattered sill of what had been a window to look out. Soon, he was firing away. Then he moved to the next window and fired some more, giving the illusion that they were all still manning their posts. "I think some of these Maras are moving away," he said.

"But look behind them," Wes said.

"Holy Toledo! Am I seeing what I think I'm seeing?"

"What's that, Al?" Fergie asked.

He dared a longer peek out the window and squinted. "Well, my aunt Gertie's girdle. They look like Puro Tango Blast to me. We're in the middle of a flipping war between two of the worst gangs in Texas."

"Way to soften it," Fergie muttered. He had at least toned down his language, but she suspected some of the ripple of fear she'd just experienced was going through Cricket and Baron like rushing streams.

Chapter Twenty-Two

Escovar watched the tail end of the Maras group scooting out of sight as they went into what looked like a full panic but could have been a ruse to lure the Tangoes their way as they rearmed.

"José, go back as fast as you can and check on the buses."

"You think this is a trap?"

"We have sprung many. We do not wish to be in one. Just go!"

José took off at a run. The buses were not so far away that Escovar and the others wouldn't know soon.

The Tango Blast mob formed one big line, except for those left behind to tend to the wounded or worse. They swept the land like a horde of locusts, just the way Escovar liked to see them working together. Here and there, they found a fallen Salvadoran who wasn't dead and fixed that. They were one big killing machine. Escovar grinned. All he had wanted was for his boys, Roberto, José, and now little Pablo, to experience the camaraderie, protection, and thrill of being a Puro Tango Blast member with the full force of cartel backings that had once made him tingle.

It was too late for Roberto, but at least José and Pablo were sharing the moment. Escovar listened. He thought he could hear less shooting. Maybe the battle was seeing its day. The Maras were moving fast, and he was tired himself of tromping across the open nothing of the ranchero. They had taken a toll, already accounting for half of the force those Salvadorans had assembled. Should they turn and go home? That would depend.

He glanced to the rear. José came running toward them as fast as he could go.

As he came up to Escovar, panting, he stopped, bent at the waist, gulping in air.

"Come on. Let's have it," Escovar said.

"Black vans. Some big, others smaller," José gasped.

"Who?"

"They were ICE and ATF."

"How many?"

"I could not know. I didn't stay to count. More vehicles were coming in. I took off to let you know. But many. I would say many."

They had not come in by air. He hadn't heard any copters. That meant they perhaps knew about the missiles. Escovar shook his head hard and made himself think. "We will see. We need a place to defend."

He looked about. All he saw in all directions was the cabin, which some of the Tangoes were already firing at. "We need that. We need to take that and hold it. We won't run from this like those Maras. We will fight."

As he said it, he was far less certain himself. The *Maras Salvadoreñas* had a fierce reputation, alleged to outfight any other gang man for man, which was why the Tangoes had brought such a great number. But they were running. Why? What did they know?

"The cabin!" he yelled. "We must take the cabin!"

One of the men near him raised one of the shoulder-held missiles at the cabin.

"No, Jorge. We need that. The farmhouse might do better but not by much. And it may already be taken. Let's get that cabin."

?

Al rose to fire out over the shattered sill of his window, taking a sweeping look at the opposition as he did. He plopped low to the floor as bullets responded, flying through the cabin to take out a lantern hanging on the other wall that had survived that long.

The battle that had already seemed nearly hopeless was getting worse. They were surrounded on three sides by a wall of Tango Blast members, and it was closing in. He and the others were fighting harder and were not giving in, but he had started expecting the worst. *This could be the end.*

He glanced around the cabin at the others and watched Baron rise and shoot out his window. Al wasn't sure he was always aiming, but his firing away helped keep those outside at bay for the time being.

Al picked out some wood splinters stuck in his forearm and brushed bits of glass out of his hair. Bo and Wes weren't saying anything about their injuries, which were worse. He rose again and saw someone running toward the cabin. He fired then saw the guy tumble to the ground with flailing limbs and not get back up.

"We've got to leave here," he said. "Any ideas?"

"They sure seem set on taking the cabin now," Wes agreed.

"I say we let them have what they want." Al popped out his spent clip and popped in another. He began to gather all the ammo he could and put it into a pack. He found a bottle of water that didn't have holes in it and slipped it in as well.

"Where will we hide?" Fergie asked. She still covered Cricket, who peeked out from under her with wide eyes.

"Bo?" Wes asked.

Bo nodded then shrugged.

"He knows a place. It's not tip-top, but if that gang wants this place, we can get out of their way by going there."

?

Walter Pagent wore his combat ATF uniform but had hoped he wouldn't need it—an idle hope, knowing the fierceness and boneheaded stubbornness of those Mara Salvatrucha gangbangers.

His phone rang.

"Yes?"

A voice came over and said simply, "They're just coming in to you."

It was Avila letting him know that the retreating Maras were entering the ranch where he waited.

Good. Also, not a single media van had rolled up outside yet. Oh, they would be present soon, like the hungry jackals they were. But for the moment, he felt freer to act. He turned and waved to his men by the trucks. Two Lenco Bearcats, armored SWAT vehicles, rolled off the beds of trucks and came up and took position before armed men in SWAT gear poured into them.

Pagent had been present in Waco when the ATF finally stormed the Mount Carmel Center of the Branch Davidians back in 1993. *What a fiasco that had been!* But he suspected the Maras would be their own undoing. Tired and animal angry, they were out in the open. He had already secured their shoulder-launch missiles and the rest of their weapons. He had enough for a weapons trafficking charge. The rest would be up to them. They were allies to the Sureños, Los Zetas, and Mexican Mafia cartels, though, so he still didn't expect a peaceful surrender.

What really rubbed his rhubarb was that the sort of stinger missiles the Maras and the Tango Blast had were manufactured in the United States, stored in America, and stolen in America.

He'd been first-line with the theft of the stinger missiles from a supposedly secret armory located in the wild somewhere near Texoma. Cases of them had disappeared. Some had appeared as far away as Mexico, during the cartel battles there. That was when he'd had to start dealing with Jaime Avila and ICE. No one knew the cartels better than Jaime, he'd been told, and the first thing Jaime had told Pagent was that he had a hunch about where some of the other missile cases had gone.

From his position with the ATF, Pagent had tracked the cases to Bob's Bangs, a small-time weapons dealer who had just gone big time in southern Minnesota. Previously, Bob Truckster had only dealt in antiquated army surplus, used weapons, and old military paraphernalia, showing up at gun shows and festivals. Suddenly, he became the big blip on Pagent's screen.

Once they'd taken him in and rattled him good, he'd gone for a plea bargain that led Pagent's ATF team to a former army reservist, Marvin Grampist, who with two friends had cracked the security at the site where the stingers were kept and had made off with more than two dozen cases of stingers, each launcher valued at close to forty thousand dollars retail to buyers.

Not wanting to call attention to himself, since he had been stationed at the site and knew how to disable the security cameras, Grampist had sold the lot wholesale to Truckster, who had contacts from gun shows, he had said, and who'd told him to let them know if he ever got his hands on something "really good."

Grampist ended up facing felony charges for probation violation—he had been out on bail for a child-rape case and had worn an electronic bracelet during the heist—possession of stolen firearms, theft of government property, selling stolen weapons, and a handful of other charges for the B and E and damages to the security apparatus at the facility.

Even with the plea deal, he was facing ten years for each charge and was probably not going to see daylight again.

Truckster, who claimed he was just doing business in a wholesome American way, was being held on nearly as many felony charges. But none of the charges and eventual penalties did anything about the serious firepower floating around both north and south of the border.

The magnitude of the crimes became apparent when a Sinaloa cartel group fired one of the missiles at a helicopter belonging to Los Zetas in a battle that took place deep on Mexican soil, close enough to the touristy parts of the Yucatan Peninsula to alarm those who valued tourism revenue dollars. That was when Pagent's path crossed that of Jaime Avila, who said he knew about the missiles and was tracking them from his end.

Neither had previously communicated about the missiles, and they both agreed to keep the chase between themselves, or they would have those suit-and-tie FBI clowns all over the trail. Heaven help them if those Bureau guys had found out there was a kidnapping in the mix, too, or he and Avila would have had their hands full, keeping them on the sidelines of a muddle that was only beginning to clear to the current battle lines.

Bob Truckster, no doubt tempted by massive piles of cartel money, had clearly sold them to both sides of this fracas. Pagent was fine if they used them on each other and wiped their sort of gangs off the face of America. But that was wishful thinking and probably not very P.C.

Pagent had possessed the intel he needed to act on the Tangoes a week before.

"Wait," Avila had advised, "unless you want some massive collateral damage in the middle of one of the biggest cities in America. Better we get them out so we only risk some lizards, snakes, a few head of cattle, and the odd rancher or so."

Few people of his acquaintance knew more about the cartels and the American gangs affiliated with them than Jaime Avila. So Pagent had waited. How Avila knew that over one hundred Tango Blast members and the missiles they were after would be heading out to this particular spot was beyond Pagent, but his intel had been damned good.

Pagent glanced over the ICE portion of the group he headed. *What a crew!* The men had the maverick look of wild-west gunslingers, with their sidearms—most of them the Sig Sauer P229Rs they'd been issued, although a few carried alternatives that they'd purchased on their own. They wore them low on their hips and with vests full of extra clips for the Colt M4 carbines or Heckler & Koch submachine guns they carried.

These men were Homeland Security's answer to fighting fire with fire when it came to cartels. They were raw and tough but far from totally undisciplined. More than anything, they resembled the early Texas Rangers, who were made up of all kinds of tough hombres able to deal with the nasties of their time. The ICE men looked every bit as ready to ride hard and shoot straight.

At any other time, they might have given Pagent reservations, but under the circumstances, he thought they might be exactly what was needed. Jaime's number-two lieutenant, Max Bellows, who would head the ICE part of the attack force supporting Pagent, looked young and brash. He wore a perpetual sneer that would have made Elvis proud and made Pagent think of the phrase "the iceman cometh." The guys looked like—and were—killers. He guessed he would soon see how they would fare against the sort of ruthless men famed for their be-headings, mutilations, and indiscriminate murders of people of all ages.

With his and part of Avila's men, he had the distinct privilege of facing a group of what some called the most dangerous gang in Amer-ica, the Mara Salvatrucha. At least this batch of Maras was without missiles and would have to face armored SWAT vehicles. He wanted to take them all alive, but that was up to them. Perhaps the survivors should adjust those three-dot tattoos they wore to mean more than just prison, death, or hospital. They should add a fourth dot once those ICE lads got a hold of them, a dot for deportation.

?

As Mauricio and his remaining men got closer to the ranch build-ings they had occupied themselves, he could see men in black SWAT outfits swarming the structures... and finding nothing, unless he count-ed the weapon stores he had been hoping to revisit so he could rearm.

They still had momentum but were heading into a bad situation. All of them could be captured or killed. The horde of Tango Blast gang-bangers behind him made retreating that way impossible.

"First, prison-hardened Tangoes, and now this." Mauricio had to make a snap decision. "Charge! Go at them. This is the day you have been practicing for."

He hung back as his recruits, some in the remaining gators and others on foot, rushed across the rough pasture and toward the buildings. After they passed, he waited until the men in black noticed them and formed up to confront the incoming Maras. Two armored vehicles rolled out at the front of the men in black.

As the two forces met, Mauricio waved for his driver to turn and take off. He, the driver, and the two men still in the back could perhaps get away, and he planned to try. He could always train more recruits. He would have to be the one to convey all that had happened to the cartel bosses, but they were used to losses as well as victories, given their way of doing business. They thrived on risk, and the story he could tell of all the forces present there would surely exonerate him.

The gator ran full-out, sometimes bouncing high as the wheels traversed bumps as well as dips and holes in the ground.

"Más rápido!" he called to the driver, even though the two in the back were bouncing higher with each pounding bump. They clung to the gator bed's sides as if their lives depended on it, and they did.

Mauricio kept glancing back. Soon, he could see no more of the buildings or the confrontation they had left behind. He kept checking, expecting to be chased. But after a while, he relaxed enough to take a deep breath. They seemed to be alone. *Now to get clear of the ranchero.*

?

The wide combined line of the Puro Tango Blast approached the cabin from three sides like the giant pinchers of a crab ready to pinch the life out of those inside.

Al watched the line of gang members get closer. "We've got to get out of here, pronto!"

Wes looked at Bo. "Lead, and we'll follow." He turned to the others. "You all are gonna have to stay as low as you can get. Recall the slither you've seen Bo use. You're gonna have to make the area snakes envious."

Al was no stranger to the crawl. He'd learned it in the military, as he suspected Bo and Wes had.

It turned out that Baron was good at imitating and following. Fergie had been in such tight situations before and got far lower to the ground than Al could manage. Little Cricket acted like it was a game and was the smallest of them to begin with, so being in the sinuous snake line was almost fun for her.

Al would normally have kidded, "Does crawling like this make my butt look big?" But he kept as silent as he could, like the others, as Bo went along the ground almost faster than the others could follow.

Tall grass, bent and brown in places, covered much of their escape. Al's knees bumped into occasional rocks, and he passed over open holes he hoped were the homes of armadillos rather than snakes. But Bo going first meant they went out and around stands of prickly pear or thicker stands of chaparral in a spread that hadn't been worked hard as a cattle ranch in some time. At least that meant no cow pies for them to encounter.

Normally, he would have hoped for some sort of diversion while they got away. But those Tangoes seemed so intent on taking the cabin that the wings of their line were closing in on it while none of them seemed to see the former occupants fifty yards out and moving fast.

Al knew the back fence of the property wasn't a vast distance away, but finding a temporary hiding place was all they could hope for now.

Shouting and shooting came from the cabin's direction. The line of those who crawled ahead of him began to dip and go down out of sight. Soon, the bottoms of Fergie's boots ahead of him went downward as well. Al followed down into the narrow, sloping walls of a rocky arroyo, a gully at least five or six feet deep, before it became a mat of thorny vegetation barely deep enough for them to hide in.

He was thinking about snakes and didn't feel better when he could see the others huddled low as Bo twisted the neck of a rattlesnake and threw it over the side of the deepening ditch. At least he couldn't see any heavy growth where they hid, though some thick vegetation formed a thorny wall just ahead as the arroyo went down farther into a groove cut by the occasional downpours in between long hot spells each summer.

He went down as far as he dared then turned to face upward. Wes crawled up past the others and squeezed past with a minimum of awkward grunts.

When he reached where Al waited, he stayed low beside him. "We'll watch from here."

"Hopefully, getting the cabin will be enough for them," Al said.

"Yeah, hopefully," Wes said. "But I doubt it."

Chapter Twenty-Three

Escovar was among those at the front when the first of his fellow Tangoes burst inside the cabin, firing away. Almost at once, the shooting stopped.

Estaban stuck his head out the open door. "Clear! It's empty in here."

Several of them swarmed, Escovar, José, and Pablo among them, then crammed inside. Jorge stuck his head inside and said, "Is too crowded in here for me. We'll form a ring of trenches around the place. You see anything like a shovel in here?"

Pablo held up a garden shovel with a shaft that had been broken halfway up. The break in the shaft looked as dirty as the rest of the shovel, so it had been that way for a long spell.

"It will have to do." Jorge grabbed what there was of the tool and started to go outside.

"See if you and the others can find any trace of where those inside went. They didn't just disappear."

"I don't know," Jorge said. "Maybe they are here still but are ghosts." He chuckled as he disappeared out the doorway.

Escovar worked his way to one of the windows through the rubble on the floor. He looked out in the direction from which they had come. He didn't see any of the men of ICE or the ATF yet. But he suspected they would be coming this way all too soon.

Around him, the other Tango Blast members were seeing to their weapons, making sure they had full clips.

He went over to the two mounds on the chairs. One chair was on its side, but the sheet still covered it. He whisked the sheets aside. "We better get these Maras outa here. They gonna start to stink real soon."

A couple of the men dragged each corpse outside, still tied to its chair. He watched out a window as they added them to a pile of brush some of the Tangoes were building as a defense wall.

Escovar looked around at the bullet-riddled walls of the cabin, where bright sunlight poked through and made beams that lit the cabin's insides in odd sprays, the way a disco ball might have. It didn't look like a very strong defense against any armed opposition, but it would have to do. It was all they had.

?

As Jorge went out the cabin door, he handed off the broken shovel he'd found to one of the men among those forming an expanding defensive perimeter by digging trenches. Some had taken loose boards from the cabin and were digging with them as best they could. He hoped the few others who had done their time at Clemens State Prison in Brazoria, as he had, were saving him some room in a trench when he got back.

For the moment, his task was to find where the occupants had gone. They'd been inside not that long ago. It wouldn't do to have them lurking around behind them. He bent low and looked for a sign. Having to stay more or less upright while the others were hunkered down exposed him somewhat but took him away from the side where he expected the men in black to hit. He didn't take long to find a displaced groove of dirt and dust where people had slithered in single file. The trail, such as it was, led away from the cabin. No attempt had been made to erase it. If he'd been looking for footprints, he would have missed the path. But it looked as though they had dragged themselves. Bent grass and a few broken twigs helped, but it wasn't an especially hard trail to follow.

But the inhabitants of the cabin must have left late and hadn't had enough time to get as far as the deer fence he could see in the far distance. With each step, he grew more wary.

He knew he was close enough when someone fired a shot in his direction. Maybe it was a warning shot, or maybe the shooter was rattled or not that good of a shot. In any case, he dropped to the ground, not giving the shooter a second chance.

"Over here!" he yelled. "I'm gonna need some help over here!"

Others of the nearest Tangoes rose and rushed to join in. Here was someone to shoot at. That eased the tension of waiting and gave them something to do. They began to fire away. They didn't want any of their enemies lurking on the back side of their defenses.

?

Baron dropped back into the arroyo after firing a shot at the man he'd seen.

Well, that was a damn fool thing to do, Al thought. Chances were good that someone would have spotted them anyway. But all his hope of them lying low until they could slip away had disappeared.

"I wish you'd waited a bit before shooting," Wes said. "At least until he was in your range."

"I didn't want to kill him. I just wanted to scare him off."

"These aren't the sort of jaspers who scare easily," Wes said. He turned to Al. "Right?"

Al didn't get a chance to answer. Other Tango Blast members came running up to form a circle around their hiding place, which was by no means a secret any longer. They began to fire toward the spot. Having them on all sides, such as they were, was going to make getting clear of the arroyo almost impossible. He could hope some of them might shoot each other, the way they were firing from multiple directions. But even that was a lot to wish.

He looked toward Fergie. He didn't want to say how hopeless their situation looked. She clung tighter to Cricket and moved her to the lowest, safest spot in the arroyo. The rim of the gully rose four to five feet above them there.

While Wes and Bo moved up to as near the top of the groove as they dared, in order to shoot at anyone who decided to come running their way, Al moved down until he was beside Fergie. He put an arm around her briefly. She nodded. They were ready to say their good-byes to each other.

Baron moved closer. "Let me hold Cricket awhile," he whispered to Fergie, "in case something happens." He handed his rifle to Fergie, which was just as well, Al figured, since it let him focus on Cricket and kept him from wasting ammunition. Though his intentions had been good, he was far from a great shot. Also, Al had a feeling that Baron didn't really want to hurt anyone, wasn't capable of it. That would serve him well elsewhere, but they needed accurate firepower to get the best of those trying to kill them.

Fergie moved closer to Al, and they embraced. He didn't much care what anyone thought just then. He wanted to hold her. They had only a moment or two before they pulled apart.

"Well, let's go help Wes and Bo repel boarders." Al struggled to grin. "What do you say?"

"Aye, aye." Fergie's voice had a rasp to it, and she rubbed at her eyes. But she checked the rifle she held, tucked the spare clip Baron had handed her inside her belt, and followed Al as high up in the arroyo as they dared.

Shots ricocheted off rocks, sending splinters of rock and showers of sand and dirt in sprays across them. When Al peeked up in a brief reconnoiter, he could see ten, maybe twelve of the Tangoes in a surrounding circle. He sure couldn't see any clear way out of their mess.

Chapter Twenty-Four

Meryl had read up on it a bit on the internet, but she didn't really know much about GSR, or gunshot residue, except what she'd heard on television shows or seen in a book somewhere. She did know it had to be on him but not on her. Maybe it would be enough just to have him holding the barrel when it went off.

She knew she had to get rid of the clothes she was wearing at the time. She could put them in a plastic bag and bury the bag as soon as possible. She got a bar of Lava soap from beneath the kitchen sink and took it into the shower, where she could scrub herself until she was pink all over—especially her hands. The act of scrubbing her hands so hard again and again would probably make her think of Lady Macbeth. But she didn't dwell on that.

She would then get dressed again and take the plastic bag of clothes out to bury it behind the pecan tree beyond the far side of the corral. As she assembled everything she thought she needed, she considered whether it would be best to call an ambulance or the sheriff's department to report that there had been a terrible accident. The sheriff's department, she guessed. Besides, Rosa, the sheriff, hadn't seemed to care much for Colin, and that might just be a help.

Today would be the best day, since Gaby was supposed to be off to town, shopping for fresh groceries.

Colin had showered after his jog and sat in his reading chair. *Perfect.* When she went into the living room, he just looked up at her from his book and grunted.

While he ignored her, she put his rifle-cleaning kit on the small table by his chair. She had already assembled the cleaning rod and put an oily rag in the end slot.

He glanced up at her out of the corner of his eye.

She took his commemorative rifle down from its mount over the fireplace mantel. A Winchester 94 lever-action .30-30 Lone Star model that he claimed was mint, though he kept it loaded and ready all the same.

"You know what my pop always said to me?" Colin lowered the book he held to his lap.

"No. What?"

"That if your first thought about a rose is its thorns, you probably shouldn't get married."

"Did he, now?"

"Okay. What's on your so-called mind?"

"Did you have anything to do with my sister's death, or was that truly an accident?"

"You're talking hogwash."

"Well, I think you wished for it, even if you didn't cause it."

"What's that matter? I'm with *you* now. Unless this is about Baron. Is it?"

Meryl tilted her head, getting a new perspective of him. *What the hell?*

His eyes opened wider as she swung the barrel of the Winchester until it was aimed at his heart. He was starting, just beginning to believe.

"What are you trying to pull? Shooting someone takes more than just wishing it done. Are you out to prove you're a Venus with a penis?" He grabbed at the barrel.

She swept the end of the gun away.

He stayed seated. "I always knew you were the bad one," he said, "but I figured I could handle that."

"Well, how's that working out?" She swung the barrel until it stayed fixed on his chest. He grabbed at it, trying to yank it out of her hands.

She pulled the trigger.

He had the most surprised look she'd ever seen on his face. Then he slowly slumped to one side.

She turned and saw Gaby staring at her.

"Madre de dios!" Gaby spun and took off at as fast a run as her short legs could muster.

?

Gaby ran across the brown tiles of the kitchen floor, where she had spent countless hours. She got to the back door that opened out onto the patio. She opened it then slammed it shut, hard and loud. Then she ran to the pantry. She had only seconds.

She reached a hand down to the right of the wooden floor, slipped her fingers inside a small slot, and lifted a trapdoor that led down to a root cellar. There were no roots there, unless she counted a few bags of potatoes. Shelves held dusty wine bottles along one wall and jars of dried herbs and spices along the other wall.

The stairway had only a half dozen steps. She rushed down then reached to close the pantry door behind her. Then she closed the trapdoor over her and lowered herself to the cement floor, where she sat trembling in the dark. She shivered and reached for her rosary to finger the beads rapidly. Steps rushed across to the door outside then came back to the pantry, even clicking across the wood above her head.

Baron knew about the root cellar, but she didn't think Señora Meryl did.

Gaby did all she could to keep from sobbing out loud. She kept her lips pressed tightly together and moved the beads faster and faster.

?

Meryl came back out of the pantry and slammed the door closed. Well, she hadn't planned on that. She had to find that woman. *Where could she go?* Meryl couldn't see her outside, but she could swear she'd heard the door slam. She opened the door and rushed out across the patio, heading for the stables, still carrying Colin's stupid rifle. She should have left it beside him, but she might need it. Even as she ran, she sought to weave a new story of how she might explain all this.

Chapter Twenty-Five

Except for the steady popping of rifle shots and strings of automatic bursts over where Jorge and a few of the other Maras were probably rubbing out whoever had been inside, the area around the cabin was quiet—ominously so.

When Escovar peeked through the gaping shattered hole that had been a window, he could see widely spread dots of black coming slowly toward the cabin. That made sense. They wouldn't dare cluster together.

Escovar waved his two sons closer. When José and Pablo huddled close to him, he bent toward them and said, "What's the worst that could happen? For me, that I go back to prison or die. But I do not wish you boys to go to prison. You would not like it there. It is not a place to be liked. So we fight. Right?"

They both nodded eagerly, clenching their weapons.

He tossed his head toward the window, where outside he'd seen the approaching feds. "They are afraid this time, too, because of those." He waved a hand toward the men outside in the trenches. Three of them still had the straps of the shoulder-launch stinger missiles over their shoulders. "That is why they cannot use their helicopters or come at us en masse. Many of them could die. They don't care that much about us, but they fear for their own numbers. So we will see. Eh?"

The two boys eased away and fidgeted their way closer to the windows, eager for the fight to begin. All their lives, they had been ready to be treated like men, and they had their chance. Escovar watched them and felt a warm glow. It would be a siege, but that meant there might be opportunities to fight and break clear. "We will see," he said again to himself. "We will see."

?

Al reached into the soft pack at his feet and took out another clip for his rifle. He held it up for Fergie to see—the last one.

She nodded, held up her spare clip, and extended it to him. He shook his head—best she keep it for the time being. She might need it when things got dicey, which would be soon.

Baron stayed huddled as low in the arroyo as he could get, covering Cricket, who peeked out around him.

Al looked around himself, taking in the sky and the bent tall brown grass outside the lip of where they crouched, and then fixed on Fergie's eyes.

The moment was one in which they said a whole lot without having to say a word.

The men shooting at them had been content to plink steadily away, probably suspecting that ammo was getting low for Al and the others. They were right about that.

Wes and Bo had certainly grown a lot in Al's estimation of them. But it wouldn't be enough in the end unless something changed. He held little hope for that.

He eased closer to Fergie and held out a hand. She reached for his and held it tightly.

He closed his eyes for a second and did a quick review of their times together. When he opened them, he saw Cricket staring at him, her eyes open wide and questioning. She seemed to be grasping for some tiny ray of hope, and he wished on everything that he could give it to her.

His ears caught a sound, or rather a diminishing of sounds, and his eyes snapped open. He had detected a change in the shooting around them.

None of the shots were slamming into the top edges of their little canyon or spraying gravel across them any longer.

He dared to peek over the lip of stone. The Tangoes on one side were pulling back, slowly and, it seemed, resentfully.

From the other direction, he caught a glimmer of a brown suit then another. They scurried and fired while coming his way, as trained troops did when in a contested war zone.

Fergie rose with her rifle.

"Hold your fire," Wes said.

The Tangoes around them on their side began to fade and ease back. Others still fired but not at the arroyo—they shot at the men in brown.

Al could clearly see the SWAT letters on their uniforms. He took his first really deep breath of air in what seemed a very long time.

As the men in brown advanced, they drove a wedge to where Al and the others crouched. Two of the masked, uniformed SWAT team members scrambled forward and tumbled into the edge of the arroyo. The bigger of them turned to aim his weapon, a Colt M4 Carbine, toward the Tangoes, who were resisting, not seeming to be willing to be pushed back.

The smaller of the SWAT team duo tugged off her mask and revealed herself as Rosa, sheriff of the county. Al had never expected to be so relieved to see her face again, but a wave of the deepest sort of thanks and appreciation swept through him.

"Don't have a whole lot of time for chit-chat," she said, "but you people are in a very bad place."

"We've got to get this girl out of here," Fergie said.

"And I've got to get my unit to join the others. There's a damn sight more of these bangers than I've ever seen or dealt with before." She turned to Al. "A guy who claims to be a pal of yours is in charge of this shindig. Some big shot in ICE."

"Jaime Avila?"

"That's the guy."

If the Immigration and Customs Enforcement people were involved, it was indeed big. Al saw a tiny, flickering ray of hope.

"Some ATF people are here as well. They couldn't use copters because of the missiles."

"What missiles?" Fergie asked.

"The big bunch of them a handful of cartels got their hands on. Everybody has been handling this whole thing carefully, very carefully. It's why I couldn't say anything. This current push is called Operation Boa, since they have to use a slow squeeze instead of just storming in here."

She looked around at each of them and ended up fixed on Baron then Cricket. "I can't protect you here. We can barely protect ourselves."

"This end is just your little piece of the action?" Fergie asked.

"Yep." She nodded. "I know when I'm in over my head. I was just hoping you retired raspberries didn't stir things up too soon, and you darn near did."

"You knew where Baron was?" Fergie's eyes opened wider.

"I had a hunch, but I couldn't act right away. Now, I can."

Al could have mentioned that Rosa had left Baron hanging out to dry for a spell, but she had clearly been playing along with the feds and maybe not enjoying that. However, she was also after clearing far bigger fish out of her county.

"We're fine with getting out of here," Al said. "Is a direction clear?"

"Sort of." Rosa took a quick look up over the rim of their hiding place. "I'll have Took show you the way. Just stay low and follow him when I say 'go.' Jaime and his men, along with some ATF guys, are tending to all kinds of Maras and Tango Blast gang members out there."

"Well, thanks," Fergie said. "We were sure up against it here."

"I'd best skedaddle," Rosa said. "There's a lot to do yet in closing down this direction. My SWAT team, such as it is, has been dying for a chance to take part in something like this, and personally, I've been chomping at the bit to do something here while your pal Avila made me wait." She stayed low as she moved away in the tall grass.

They formed up, ready to take off. Baron and Cricket moved to the middle, where the others could cover them better.

Cricket tugged on the lower edge of Al's shirt. He turned to look at her.

"Took is Bo's brother," she said. Neither of the two men had said a word yet, even to each other—a couple of real stone lions on the library stairs.

"Really? I just figured they went to elocution school together."

Cricket tilted her head and gave him a quizzical look.

Rosa popped her head up out of the brown grass near them again. "Okay. Go, y'all, and don't stop unless Took does."

With Took and Bo up at the front, Wes right behind them, Al and Fergie herded Baron and Cricket along as they all bent and took off in crab-like scrambles toward the property's back fence.

No one rose to shoot at them. Al saw a crumpled form here and there, so the path had been cleared. That didn't mean that the Tangoes couldn't swarm their way again at any second when the chaos stirred up to a new frenzy, so all of them stepped lively, while staying as low as they could.

Chapter Twenty-Six

"In here," Rudolpho Johnson, Jaime's number-one ICE lieutenant, yelled to him while leaning out the open door of one of the yellow school buses.

Jaime Avila climbed up the short stairs inside and followed the man in SWAT team black all the way to the back of the bus. On the floor, he saw the two open and emptied crates that had each held two of the shoulder-launch stinger missiles that had cost him the chance to ride a copter into the fray.

He took out his cell phone and punched in the number of Walter Pagent, his counterpart who led the ATF's effort. When he got an answer, he said, "All I've got here is empty crates, Walter."

"Well, all the crates here were still full. We're doing what we can with the Maras, who were coming back to their roost, and we have most of them contained."

"Most of them? Did some get clear?"

"We don't know yet. Hard to tell how many there were in the first place. We'll know more when we vigorously interrogate some of the ones we've captured."

"Well, if you can spare any of your men or mine, can you get a hustle on to come this way? And stay widely spread out. These Tango guys are heavily armed and are full of attitude. I'd leave your armored vehicles behind, or they'll be targets for missiles."

To Rudolpho, he called, "See about the keys in the other bus. I can see they left them in this one." The Tangoes had probably hoped for a quick win and a speedy getaway.

Rudolpho came back to where Jaime stood on the bus's steps with the door open.

"Yep. The keys are in that one too."

"Good. I want you to get drivers for each to bring them up and park them parallel to where those Tango Blast are hunkering down. Get three of your snipers ready to put on top of each."

"Won't these Tangoes think to shoot at the buses with their remaining missiles?"

"They might. But I suspect knowing they'll need the buses if they're ever to make an escape will make them hesitate. All we need is a second or two of an edge."

"If you say so."

"Make it happen." When Jaime stepped out of the bus, he waved for those Rudolpho wasn't commandeering to follow him and join the others advancing on the Tango Blast holdouts.

He looked out across the former cattle ranch, toward parts of it too far to see from where he stood. Somewhere out there, Al Quinn and those with him were in the thick of things. "Well, Al, I've seen you get out of some pretty nasty messes, you old rascal. I sure hope you can get yourself clear of this one."

?

Meryl felt ready to tear her hair out. She had gone back and checked every room in the house then went out to the stables again. No one was in the bunk area, so she checked each stall inside the stable. *Where the hell had Gaby gone?*

At one end of the stable, bales of hay were stacked up against the wall and up into a loft. She leaned the rifle against a wooden post and went up to the loft, wrenched a pitchfork out of a bale of hay, and used it to stab at a pile of hay. "Where are you? Where the hell are you hiding?"

She climbed back down the wooden ladder, picked up the rifle, and kept looking. She was in a tight time quandary. She needed to call the sheriff as soon as possible to report the "accident" in which Colin shot himself while cleaning his rifle. But first, she needed to find and quiet Gaby. *But where the hell is she?*

?

Escovar stood just inside the gaping hole of a former window when his Tango Blast friends began to fire on the approaching ICE and ATF teams that were spread into a wide but tightening net of individuals. Once they got close enough together, perhaps it would be possible to take out a great number of them with a missile. For the time being, they were too far apart and too far away even for accurate shooting.

Then the two buses rolled out and pulled sideways, facing the trenches the Tango Blast members were scrambling to dig. Escovar shook his head. *Are those ICE agents taunting me and the others?* Then he watched men climb up onto the tops of the buses, at least three on each bus, and sprawl into positions. *Snipers!* "Shoot at them! Get them! The men on the buses!" he yelled as loudly as he could.

The three remaining missile launchers were out among the Tangoes in the trenches. If he had one, he would fire it. The range was still too far for accurate shooting with their rifles.

But those ICE agents were cheating. He watched as one by one, some of the frontline Tangoes fell. Those damned feds were using their snipers to a devastating advantage. *Not fair. Not fair at all.* They could pick off individuals from far beyond the range of the average rifle holder.

He was about to tell the others huddled in the cabin to be careful. As he was turning to speak, he saw José peering out the next window space. "No—" he started to shout.

Even as his mouth opened, José's head jerked, and a spray of red flew back into the room. His son dropped into a crumpled pile on the cabin floor.

"No! No!" Escovar did shout it that time, but it was far too late.

His blood boiled, and his mind went into a blinding red haze of rage.

Clenching his rifle tightly, he pushed his way through the cabin and charged out the door, looking in the direction of the advancing small black figures. He roared and began to run. He headed straight for the nearest Tango Blast member holding one of the stinger missile launchers. *If he could just get to it, he would show them.*

As he passed between the others, most sprawled on the ground or sticking up out of hastily dug trenches, they yelled, "Stop. Stop, you fool!" at him, but all of their caution was lost on him.

He didn't spot any of the launchers among his fellow Tangoes. Those holding them must be hunkered down, since they were the prime targets for the snipers. So he ran past all of them.

He ran and he ran, passing the last of his men. Soon, he was running alone toward the enemy through the tall brown grass.

The first bullet hit him low in the pelvis. He staggered but kept trying to run. The next hit him in the shoulder, and then two or three in a row from various directions slammed into his chest. He thought he was running and running but then felt the ground smash into him hard as he crumpled into it. Then he felt nothing at all.

?

Mauricio's gator was going flat-out, nearly hitting its top-end capacity of sixty miles an hour and bouncing the men inside almost out of it with each hard bump, when it began to sputter and slow.

"Faster," Mauricio said.

The driver shrugged and pointed at the dial on the dash. The gas indicator was on empty. The gator slowed and finally came to a stop.

They got out. Mauricio looked around. At least he couldn't see anyone chasing them. They weren't that far from the back cattle fence, but he and his three remaining men were on foot.

He shook his head and began to limp toward the fence line. The three men with him reached to take out their rifles and what ammo packs they still had. The small group started off through the tall, swaying brown grass, with Mauricio muttering to himself as he limped along.

Chapter Twenty-Seven

Al heaved a big sigh when they came to the gate in the deer fence at the back of Darren and Dewey's ranch. It was closed but unlocked. At its base, a rusted chain lay in twisted, broken lengths on the ground. From what he could tell, someone had taken a short length of rebar they'd found and had twisted it round and round until the too-thin and tired chain had popped, mangling several links.

He glanced toward Took, and Wes nodded. That was probably how the sheriff and her men had gotten in. She probably carried a warrant as well. But Took had done the job on the chain.

Once they were through the gate, Took paused to tug off the SWAT team mask covering his face. He rubbed at the patina of sweat on his face. Neither he nor Bo was ever going to talk anyone to death, but Al was glad to have both of them along.

Wes took the lead and headed toward where they'd tied the horses he and Bo had ridden next to Diablo.

Al regretted their sending the other horses back.

"Water?" Cricket said as soon as they got to where the horses stood waiting. She extended a hand.

Al took out the bottle he'd stowed in his pack and held it out to Cricket.

She cupped one hand and poured a little water in and let Diablo drink from her hand. She went to the other two horses and did the same for them. "They've been standing out here in the heat a while. It's only fair if they're to get us back."

"We'd better get a move on," Fergie said.

"We might could double up for the first stretch, if we only had one more horse," Wes said. "But these three can't go the whole distance with all of us on."

"Let's just get away for now," Al said.

There were three horses and seven of them.

"It's tricky to impossible, given the math," Wes said. "Plus, a couple of us are pretty hefty." He glanced toward Bo and Took.

"You can go back to your team, Took," Al said.

He shook his head.

"He's probably on orders to see we get to safety before he can go back," Wes said.

Al glanced toward Fergie. She shook her head. Neither of them had heard either Bo or Took say a word. Perhaps theirs was some sort of genetic trait, but he had never seen anything quite like it. For a second or two, he wondered if they were twins, but that was a topic he didn't want to touch at all.

"I'll walk with you and Took at first," Al said to Wes. "Baron can ride behind Cricket, and Bo should ride, since he's the most injured. Fergie can mount the remaining horse."

"You could ride behind me, Al," Fergie said.

"Let's try it with me on foot for now," Al said, "to be fair."

Once those riding were mounted, they started off, slowly at first, but each step was one farther away from the shooting they could still hear behind them.

"Boy, it's sure going on back there." Cricket turned in her saddle to look toward the ranch they'd left behind.

"Let's just be glad we're moving away from it," Baron said from where he rode behind her on Diablo.

They rode as quietly and steadily as they could. Bo and Took sometimes glanced around then at each other, taking in more than Al could see. Sometimes, Took slipped off to look out into the fields they were passing. Their silent communication added to the eerie silence of the ride so far. Al heard just the slow clopping of hooves on the hard ground.

Each of them glanced back now and then to where the steady crackle of gunfire suggested the fight back there was far from finished.

Al had been over this wash of a trail more than once and knew when they were about halfway across the back end of the ranch the Maras had occupied. They would begin to see the makeshift airstrip soon.

But when they crested the next small rise, he didn't get the time or the opportunity to look off to the right. Four men burst out in front of them, and three of them held automatic rifles.

He and Wes were in the front, on foot. Took had slipped to the back of the group to have another look around. The others were still on the horses. He glanced back. Cricket was reining in Diablo, with Baron still sitting behind her. Fergie rode a horse by herself. Took had been with them a moment or two ago. *Where the hell had he gone? Had he started back the way he was supposed to have done?*

"The horses, señors. We have need of your horses." The stocky, heavily tattooed man in the middle didn't have a rifle in hand, but he kept one hand on the hilt of a machete in a sheath at his side.

Al glanced toward Fergie. She was mentally answering the same question he had about why these Maras hadn't just opened fire. They didn't want to harm the horses, which they needed. Nor did they wish to hit the women, who could provide entertainment. Cricket might even be a product for their human trafficking activities. She was light enough to ride away with them as they made their getaway.

"I am Mauricio. You will do as I say. The horses," the Maras leader said again. "First, lower your weapons to the ground. Then bring the horses to us, slowly."

The others dismounted, and all put their guns down in the dirt. Bo and Al each took the reins of a horse. Al held the reins to Diablo. Wes took the reins of Fergie's horse once she was on the ground. Bo had kept the reins of the horse he'd been riding. The three of them began to move forward.

Al would not have been surprised if they were gunned down where they walked. Only the prospect of the horses being injured probably prevented that. These were ruthless killers, and the sounds of the distant battling only underscored how desperate they might be.

He was thinking as hard as he could. A Salvadoran with an M-16 stood on either side of Mauricio. One of them stood much farther off to one side, way out of range for any of them to try anything. All of their eyes glittered. Their hands held the rifles with no quiver. They looked ready—even eager—to shoot.

All the math he had ever learned was of no use there. Al had to figure the scenario. The moment they handed over the horses, they were dead, maybe all of them. The Maras may well have valued moving quickly over even messing with a woman and a girl. They were known kidnappers and dabblers in human trafficking, and a young girl might have tempted them at other times. But the men were on the run.

Bo and Wes held their reins extended. Each of the men holding rifles reached with their left hands but didn't lower their weapons.

In a burst, Al dropped the reins he held and ran as fast as he could with his head lowered. He rammed headfirst into Mauricio's belly.

He expected at any second to hear shots and feel them slamming into him. Maybe the others could get away. It was a thread and a damned slim one, but people didn't get second chances with the likes of those gangbangers.

Out of the corner of his eye, he saw a black blur smash into the guy who held a rifle off trail on the far right. He might have hesitated so as not to hit any of his own gang, but Took had crept close enough to leap in.

Bo easily smashed his man to the ground and wrested away his rifle. Wes was having a harder time grappling for control of the rifle with the other Salvadoran, but Baron ran in to grab at the gun and help. They piled on him and took him to the ground, ripping away the rifle from him.

Mauricio was gasping for air but managed to pull his machete from its sheath and straightened himself upright, holding it high.

Al grabbed Mauricio's wrist with both hands and was wrestling for control of the machete hand when Fergie flashed in and, kicking with all her strength, connected with the fork of Mauricio's thighs in a hard thud as she split the uprights. It would have been a field goal on any professional football field. Al winked at her.

Mauricio's eyes shot open wide as he let go of the machete. He crumpled to the ground, his hands going to hold his crotch.

Bo held his man down. Took was just finishing binding his man with the kind of black-plastic zip ties law enforcement often used instead of handcuffs.

He handed a couple to Bo as he went past. Then he gave Wes and Baron a hand in tying up the guy they still wrestled with. The fight was over the minute Took stepped in and brought the hammer of his fist down on the man's head.

Took came over with a couple of the strips they could use on Mauricio, who still lay crumpled to the ground, not letting go of his crotch.

"A woman," he said. "A *pendeja* does this to me."

Fergie looked over to Cricket. "Say what you will about the martial arts, but that's always a good go-to move if some guy won't leave you alone."

Took was on his phone, so he *was* able to speak. He stepped away from where they could hear. Perhaps Rosa was one of the few people in the world, aside from Bo, to ever have heard his voice.

When he hung up, he nodded in the direction they'd been headed.

Wes looked at Bo. He understood.

"He says we're to go on," Wes said to Al and Fergie. "He's reported the capture of the head of the Maras, and he'll wait for others to come take them away."

Al shook his head. "Well, I guess we'd best get a move on before you guys talk yourselves to death."

The little band started off again. As he passed him, Al patted Took on the shoulder. It felt like tapping the side of a small mountain. But Took grinned, and Al looked toward Bo, who wore a matching grin.

Chapter Twenty-Eight

"We're sure going pretty slowly," Fergie said. She glanced back to where the noise of battle was getting louder, far from quieting down.

"We're going carefully," Wes said.

Al glanced to the ranch the Maras had occupied, which they were nearly past, then looked behind them. "That fight is breaking down into chaos. Anything can happen when that many people are desperate and don't quite know what to do."

Fergie eased her horse closer and said softly to Cricket, "I hope all this hasn't given you a bad impression about people from other countries."

Cricket shook her head. "I know the difference between the many good Latino people and those men, who are just bad and out to hurt others."

Fergie had always believed that the mark of maturity in a person was the ability to see the big picture. Little Cricket sure had a measure of that. She knew what she wanted to do in life—help others or animals—and she was careful not to judge rashly. That was more than Fergie could say for a lot of people.

"We all can be good or bad," Cricket said. "Dad thought his friends Darren and Dewey were good. We know better now."

"How do you feel about that?" Fergie asked Baron.

"I couldn't be prouder," Baron said.

?

Jaime's lieutenant, Rudolpho, eased up beside where he looked through field glasses at Tango Blast members in trenches he'd spotted on the ranchland.

"Should we make a big push now?" Rudolpho asked.

Jaime shook his head without lowering the binoculars. "This is siege and trench warfare now. Be patient. Let your snipers do their thing."

"Except for that one madman running right out at us, the bulk of the Tangoes seem content to hunker down and wait," Rudolpho said, "even though they have to see the net tightening down on them from every side."

Jaime's phone rang. He answered it when he saw it was Sheriff Rosa calling.

"This side is secure now," she said.

"Did you see anything of my friends?"

"Indeed I did. Al and Fergie were alive and kicking when I last saw them. They succeeded in getting Baron Fieldings clear of those Maras. I'll have to ask them later how they managed that."

"They work in mysterious ways," Jaime said. "Were they okay?"

"They were alive when Took or I last saw them. In the middle of all that's going on here, that's saying something."

As soon as he hung up, the phone rang again.

"Walter Pagent here. The bulk of our ATF and your ICE forces that had been on the Maras ranch with me are headed your way to cut off the rear and support you. They're just crossing over into Darren and Dewey's ranch and should be in position very soon."

"What about you?"

"I've got to do a pickup here, and I'll be right there in the mix. Your number-two lieutenant, Max Bellows, is heading the group already on its way to you. It'll be better to have them in place if this turns into the full-scale battle I expect."

Jaime looked at his watch. *It shouldn't be long, one way or the other.*

Chapter Twenty-Nine

Gino could see the ranch's buildings ahead. He glanced down at his gas gauge. The needle was almost touching the E—he was nearly out. Surely, there would be some gasoline at a place like this. He needed a full tank before he could ease out to the highway and make his getaway. Since he saw all those ICE and ATF agents at the ranch where they were being trained, he'd changed his mind about going back to help the other Maras. Just hitting the highway and getting away was starting to sound pretty good.

He watched for any movement, anyone coming out to greet him or try to shoo him off. Not a soul emerged from any of the buildings. He put the bike on its kickstand and turned off the motor. He waited in the quiet for a moment then slid the short shotgun out from under his leg, dismounted, and started across the patio and toward the house.

Any fuel was probably kept in the other buildings, but he wanted to see if anyone was around, and he was hungry and thirsty.

?

Meryl first heard and then saw the motorcycle approaching the ranch house from across the open field. "What new fresh hell is this?" she muttered and ducked back inside the stable.

The biker slowed as he neared the buildings. He seemed to be looking around. She could see he wore gang colors and looked like evil itself on the back of that bike. She clenched the rifle she held tighter. *When will this madness end?* She still had to find Gaby, take care of her, and call the sheriff. Everything she had planned was coming unraveled.

She shook her head with the awareness that she was going to have one helluva time getting all this back together the way she had planned.

?

Fergie watched Al take step after plodding step. He rubbed at the sweat running down his forehead. His boots had to be hurting. None of them had any water, though she was glad Cricket had given what was left to the horses.

"Why don't we switch? You should ride awhile," she said.

They moved slowly across the outside reaches of Meryl's spread, and that meant looking out for cow pies as well as holes in the ground. She watched Al make a special effort to breathe in the smell of the pastures and hay fields, seeming to welcome every whiff.

"We'll get there," he said.

Wes had tromped right along beside him and had never said a word in complaint.

The sun beat down on them. Fergie was hot and exhausted, emotionally as well as physically, and Al had to have been much more so. She could barely stand to watch the two of them on foot, pushing themselves to take each step.

"Couldn't we double up now, just until we get to the ranch?" she asked.

Wes looked up at her, his face darker from under the shade of his hat brim. "I know these horses, Fergie, and they're plumb tuckered. They've been out in the heat with almost no water and little to eat. If someone was tearing our way and chasing after us just now, I might agree. But I'll not hurt or kill a horse just to make things easier for the likes of us." He nodded toward Al.

Fergie didn't know what to say. Not for the first time, she had reason to ponder how she had horribly misjudged her former classmate.

"We could send Cricket ahead to get horses for you two," Baron said.

"We don't want to expose her to anything until we've checked to see if it's safe first," Al said.

"But this is home. It's safe here," Cricket said.

"When something wild is going on like we've just experienced," Fergie said, "we have no way of knowing it's truly over or safe until we've checked everything. Al's right, though I hate to see him walk and wear off the last of his boot soles."

"I can always buy new boots," Al said. "But none of *you* are replaceable." He was looking at Fergie. She blushed just a little.

"Who are you going to rush to first when we get to the house? Meryl or Gaby?" Fergie asked, to keep Cricket busy.

"Gaby," Cricket said.

"Oh?"

"I spend the most time with her. My auntie Gran is busy lots of the time."

Fergie glanced toward Al. He merely shrugged and kept plodding along.

?

Jaime looked out across the neglected pastures and toward the Tango Blast horde still sprawled in the waves of tall brown grass, waiting. The confrontation had entered a time of a pregnant pause. Except for a rare shot now and then, mostly from his own team's snipers, the front on both sides was quiet. The Tangoes were probably counting their rounds and making sure their guns were loaded and ready. He estimated that they might have lost a dozen or more so far. Hard to tell if that softened them to reason or hardened them against it. It would have been a fine time for some air support but not as long as some of those missiles were still around.

Jaime sure wished he could use a copter or two. He would normally have asked to speak to a leader, too, but not with the likes of these Puro Tango Blast gangbangers.

"This prison-fostered lot like to say they have no clear leader," Jaime said to Rudolpho, "but they have the occasional spark plug, someone who drives them forward. When that tomfool who came rushing at us fell, a good deal of their spirit and spunk may have fallen with him. We can hope for that."

"On the other hand, that man's death may have only steeled the others," Rudolpho said. "They are quieter, and that is not a good thing."

Jaime shrugged. If one or two of them had a cell phone, and if he had a number to call, they might negotiate. "Where did your snipers train?"

"Three were trained initially at Fort Bragg, where I taught. Two came through Fort Benning. Top marks. One did the SEAL school and was an instructor there for a spell. All have seen more than one hitch of active duty overseas."

"How good are they?"

"The best. Why?"

"Because our lives will depend upon them. Get one of the armored cars ready."

"Aren't you worried they'll send a missile at it?"

"Not if your men are as good as you say they are."

"They are." Rudolpho slipped away for a moment.

Less than five minutes later, Jaime was climbing into one of the Lenco Bearcat armored SWAT vehicles. As it pulled out to the front, between the two school buses, bullets pinged off its sides. Men inside returned the fire, as did the snipers on top of the buses. The vehicle turned sideways. When it stopped, Jaime asked, "Ready?"

Rudolpho nodded. He stood at Jaime's side with a bullhorn—it was standard procedure to try to negotiate peace first.

Jaime lifted the field glasses that hung around his neck and scanned the open field, where men crouched in makeshift trenches. Some of them might opt for prison over death. The Tangoes were slightly more businesslike than the Maras. If he could do what he had to without getting any more of his men wounded, that would be a victory of sorts too.

He lowered the binoculars, took the bullhorn, and pointed it out to where he could be best heard. Even inside the vehicle, he was wearing body armor, as were Rudolpho and the other ICE agents. *Well, he would see.*

He spoke slowly and carefully, first in English then in Spanish.

"Members of Puro Tango Blast. We are gathered in great force against you, and we now vastly outnumber you. We are well armed and well fed. We have supplies and support. You have none of these."

The shooting slowed. Only a shot or two bounced a bullet off the hard metal sides of the vehicle. They mattered little. One of the missiles could matter a great deal more.

He paused, thinking he heard murmuring coming from the trenches and those sprawled around the cabin.

"Further, we have captured the few remaining Maras not killed in your conflict. And their leader, Mauricio, is in our custody. That fight is over, and you have won a victory over them. But you cannot win here. I repeat, you cannot win."

He gave them a few moments. The murmuring increased, with perhaps some dissent, but he sensed the mood was changing. When the sound of them speaking to each other began to lessen, he lifted the bullhorn.

"You have to decide whether you wish to live and savor your victory or whether you'll fight... and perhaps die." He was after one specific response, so he waited. The one big uncertainty was those damned missiles, and he wanted to turn that into a certainty for his men and himself.

Jaime knew he was taking a huge risk. If one of those remaining stinger missiles was fired at him or either of the buses, it could be the end of his career and of everything else, including his life.

But the person holding the launcher had to stand and aim. He watched for them to try.

The moment the first one did, a sniper dropped him to the ground like a bag of sand.

If one of the Tangoes went to get the launcher to try again, the same thing would happen to him.

Jaime braced himself and watched the moment play out. The margin of error was fine, but it lessened as the snipers identified where each launcher was and fixed their sights on the spots. Three more times with one launcher and once with another, men tried to stand and aim until the damned things became hot potatoes no one dared to touch.

That and the fact that not everyone had experience or knowledge operating them soon took a toll. The men were crazy but not suicidal.

The wait began in earnest and was as stressful to Jaime as crash-landing a plane. Tick. Tick. Tick. They were the longest, most elastic seconds of his life.

?

Mauricio dragged one toe in the dirt and gravel and stumbled on purpose, Rosa thought.

"Step lively there." She glowered at him.

Six of her deputies, one with a bandage on one arm and another limping from where a bullet had grazed the outside of one calf, herded the Maras leader and three of his men along. They had run a rope through their arms, with their handcuffed wrists holding that in place, and were marching them in single file toward the armored vehicle coming their way across the back end of the property the Maras had occupied. The ATF agents inside would take Mauricio and his men off her hands. She was eager to get back to her team and ensure everyone was okay.

Mauricio was in the lead, and he tripped again. He had been limping and had griped about pain in his crotch. Rosa just said, "Faster."

Mauricio glared at her and started to yell in rapid Spanish.

"In English," she said. "They insist on that in the prison system, where you're headed."

"Hey, you have to be nice to me," he muttered.

"Really?" She glanced toward Took, who slapped the flat of his hand across the back of Mauricio's head.

When Mauricio snapped his head toward him, Took extended a foot. Mauricio tripped over it and fell face-first onto the dirt, just inches away from a young barrel cactus.

Took reached down with one hand and jerked the Salvadoran back to his feet.

"*Ay, caramba.*" Mauricio shook his head.

"In English," Rosa reminded him.

"*Vete al carajo!*" he snapped.

The armored vehicle pulled up, and Rosa's little caravan stopped and waited.

Walter Pagent himself led the ATF agents who came to take over the Maras prisoners.

"I'll give you a ride back to your group, Rosa," he said. "We're all apt to be needed, every man jack of us."

"You know," Rosa said to Walter as she and her men climbed into the armored vehicle, "we're just lucky those Maras with him were mostly young, raw recruits. Had there been that many battle-scarred and desperate Salvadorans, the fight on that ranch would still be going on."

Walter nodded.

"*Pendeja.*" Mauricio glared up at her from where he and the others sat on the floor with handcuffs fastened low to the vehicle's interior.

She looked down at him without a bit of pity. "Your men lost thanks to being abandoned by a coward of a leader. That's just something that is liable to slip out when you're in jail or later, when you're in prison. I suspect the other inmates are going to be apt to disrespect you over that. You can save your foul language and see how it works on them."

?

Jaime waited and waited in relative silence—there wasn't even an occasional pop of a gun for a long stretch. But he could hear one or two of them mumbling. Soon, the murmuring picked up again in earnest. He nodded to Rudolpho, although it was too soon to smile yet. He'd been sucker punched before by gangs like those.

One of the men on the ground had tied a white handkerchief to the end of his rifle. He lifted it and waved it. Another white flag waved in the window of the cabin. Then more of the men joined in. Those who had nothing white merely stood and lowered their weapons to the ground. They all began to move his way.

Off in the distance, birds rose and fluttered left then right, as if they had been waiting for a chance to stir again.

Jaime took out his cell phone and called Walter. "It's over," he told him. "It's over. Now bring your men in closer, and let's start rounding them up. Maybe it's a good thing they brought buses, eh?" He let Walter relay the order to Max Bellows, so it all remained a team effort.

Inside, he tingled with excitement and deep relief at not having to play this out with heavy bloodshed on both sides. He'd been in some awful, awful fights with such men, and this had to have been one of his greatest victories.

He watched as members of his and the ATF group led strings of the gang members his way with their hands on their heads, while others gathered up the weapons, putting them in a pile. They recovered the rest of the shoulder-launch stinger missiles first and hustled them away separately.

Rudolpho let out a long and loud breath. "I'm surprised that worked."

"Me too." Jaime glanced toward him. "I was braced for a full-out battle with heavy losses. I could live with the losses on their side but not on ours."

"What if your approach hadn't worked?"

"Then we'd probably still be in the middle of one helluva toe-to-toe battle here."

"Taking out the Maras should end some of the weapons trafficking of M-16s coming in from South America," Rudolpho said, "and with the Tangoes, we recovered the rest of the missing stinger missiles, all with a minimum of casualties. That sure ought to tickle your ATF pals. And it's a belly punch to the cartels... for now."

"We both know how long that will last."

Rudolpho shrugged. The sight of so many gang members with their hands in the air made him smile in spite of himself, though.

"Give some credit to the fact that these men were pretty played out after their dustup with the Maras, never an easy conflict," Jaime said. "But I couldn't be happier."

He could imagine Walter and a handful of his ATF men coming his way in one of the armored vehicles, and Walter would be grinning. The local sheriff, Rosa, wherever she and her men were after Walter dropped her off, was probably grinning too.

But Jaime watched the prisoners being led his way, and suddenly he was tired to the core of his bones.

He'd been lucky that time. Damned lucky. Maybe next time, he wouldn't be. They were in a longtime war with such people, and the money and power were stacked against them.

The men being rounded up were dangerous enough, and he was grateful that they'd surrendered, since the chances had been just as likely that they would have fought to their deaths. Yet they were mere pawns in a bigger, sadder game, and maybe so was he.

Aw, what the hell? Tonight, he would have a stiff drink or two and sleep restlessly. Tomorrow, it would be more of the same all over again.

He sighed, took the field glasses off his neck, and handed them to Rudolpho, who looked back at him with a puzzled expression.

Chapter Thirty

When they could see the ranch building, Fergie felt the old tug of a horse smelling its barn and wanting to go faster. But Wes and Al were walking at a snail's pace. The hike had been a long and exhausting one for them, so the group moved more slowly than she would have liked as they reached the buildings at last.

The moment they were beside the stable, Cricket hopped off her horse and handed the reins up to Bo. She took off at a run for the back door of the house.

While she was still running flat-out for the door, Fergie spotted the motorcycle resting on its kick stand. "How did that get there?"

She got it a second later.

"Don't go in there!" Fergie shouted.

Cricket rushed in the back door anyway.

Fergie dismounted, and she and Al were heading toward the back door when Gino came out, holding Cricket tightly with his left hand while waving a short double-barreled shotgun with his right.

Baron still sat on the back of his horse. "Let her go!" he yelled. "She's just a little girl!"

Neither Fergie nor Al could get to their pistols in time. Gino had his machete if he had to use up his two shots.

Meryl came out of the stable, walking steadily toward them, and she was holding a rifle.

Gino swung the barrel of the shotgun toward her but seemed reluctant to use up either of his shots. "Stay there, lady. Drop that rifle."

The back door opened again, and Gaby stuck her head out and yelled, "Watch out. She kill Mister Colin!"

"Not now, Gaby," Meryl said.

She raised the rifle and pointed it at Gino.

"Don't hit Cricket!" Baron yelled.

Gino's eyes flicked toward him, then he pulled one of the two triggers.

Meryl flew backward off her feet to plop onto the flagstone surface. Then she slowly lay back and let go of the rifle.

Baron was already off his horse and running flat-out. He slammed into Gino, wrenching Cricket loose from his grasp.

Fergie and Al ran from where they had stood.

Gino squeezed the other trigger, but the gun was pointed at a slightly upward angle.

Al smashed into Gino next and kept him from drawing out the machete he was reaching toward.

Fergie jumped in and grabbed a flailing arm. "Get some rope or wire!"

Gaby rushed inside and came out with a coil of what looked like clothesline.

"That'll do."

"You're the junior cowgirl here, Fergie. Do you want to truss him up?"

Al held Gino in a hammerlock. He snarled and tried to bite while Fergie tied his ankles.

Al flipped him over like a pancake and twisted one arm up behind his back. Fergie grabbed the other arm and tied his wrists together.

Gino let go a string of curses in Spanish and English until Al untied the blue bandana from around his neck and handed it to Fergie. She used it to gag the cussing Salvadoran.

"I doubt we made a friend here," Fergie said, and she got to her feet with a hand from Al, pushing up from the flagstone patio with the other hand.

They crossed the patio.

Cricket and Baron crouched beside where Meryl lay. Baron had yanked off his shirt and held it to her chest. Blood was already seeping through.

"I'm sorry, son. I got my values crossed." Her face grew paler, and her lips quivered.

"Where's Colin?"

"I'll be meeting him soon enough."

"I told you, she kill Mister Colin." Gaby pointed toward Meryl.

"Auntie Gran..."

"Just Gran. It's just Gran," she gasped, her breath as thin as wisps of silk. "I'll always be your Gran." She reached a hand toward Cricket, but it fell to the ground. Her head rolled over to one side.

Baron reached down to close her eyes. "I forgive you. I forgive you, Mom."

Cricket was crying so hard that Baron stood and carried her off to the end of the patio, where he lowered her onto the hanging swing, sat close beside her, and talked in low tones.

Fergie could hear a siren approaching in the distance. Gaby must have managed to call while she was still inside the house. The approaching sheriff's cruiser was going to be too late.

Chapter Thirty-One

Al watched the open pastures and wooded patches of land roll past as they grew closer to Austin. Soon, they would be around the outside of the city and in Texas hill country, at his place. "It sure feels good to be going home."

He glanced toward Fergie, who seemed to be savoring driving her own car, homeward bound. She smiled without turning her head.

"It was a joy to know Baron will have his ranch back and that Cricket, Gaby, Wes, and Bo will be back to normal, at least after the funeral," Fergie said. "That's a tough thing for a little girl to face."

"She seemed like a pretty resilient gal to me," Al said. "Kids bounce back better than you'd think. Having things back the way they were on the ranch will help—that and a few hard rides on Diablo."

The sound of asphalt rasping along beneath them and the constant changes in scenery they passed relaxed him. She wasn't humming, but she might as well have been.

"You did a smacking good job on your first case where you were boss. Good for you."

She chuckled. "Sure, if you don't count the guy who hired me getting killed."

"That was none of your doing."

"He wasn't going to pay me anything, anyway, the tightwad."

"He's cured of that."

"At least Baron promised to send me a nice check as soon as everything is settled and the ranch is all his again."

"Good for him," Al said, "and for you. But do you think he will remember in a few years who he has to thank for being free?"

"He'll only have to glance at his left hand for a reminder of the events," Fergie said. "And as for us, what do we care if we get the credit or not?"

"I guess."

"People don't always get remembered for the things they think they will," Al said. "I understand Mark Twain thought his book on Joan of Arc would be what made him remembered."

"Really? I didn't even know he'd written one on her."

"There you go."

He listened to the sound of their tires on the road and watched a ranch roll by.

"Do you think you'll miss riding horses?" she asked.

"My butt won't."

"Still a little tender?"

"Like I said, it'll be good to be home again."

"Hmm. You're right about that."

They rolled along for a few more miles. The buildings of Austin came into sight as they started around it. "Have you ever thought of making it more permanent?" he asked.

"It what? Make what permanent?" she asked.

"Us."

Her head snapped toward him. "Are you proposing, you old rascal, you?"

"Maybe. I might be."

"Well, yes. Before you have a moment to change your mind. Yes, yes, yes!"

Also by Russ Hall

An Al Quinn Novel
To Hell and Gone in Texas
A Turtle Roars in Texas
Throw the Texas Dog a Bone
A Shot in the Texas Dark
Making It Rain in Texas
Never Look Back in Texas

Standalone
Al Quinn Mysteries - Collection 1

Watch for more at www.russhall.com.

About the Author

Russ Hall is author of fifteen published fiction books, most in hardback and subsequently published in mass market paperback by Harlequin's Worldwide Mystery imprint and Leisure Books. He has also co-authored numerous non-fiction books, most recently *Do You Matter: How Great Design Will Make People Love Your Company* (Financial Times Press, 2009) with Richard Brunner, former head of design at Apple, *Now You're Thinking* (Financial Times Press, 2011), and *Identity* (Financial Times Press, 2012) with Stedman Graham, Oprah's companion.

His graduate degree is in creative writing. He has been a nonfiction editor for major publishing companies, ranging from HarperCollins (then Harper & Row), Simon & Schuster, to Pearson. He has lived in Columbus, OH, New Haven, CT, Boca Raton, FL, Chapel Hill, NC, and New York City. Moving to the Austin area from New York City in 1983.

He is a long-time member of the Mystery Writers of America, Western Writers of America, and Sisters in Crime. He is a frequent judge for writing organizations.

In 2011, he was awarded the Sage Award, by The Barbara Burnett Smith Mentoring Authors Foundation—a Texas award for the mentoring author who demonstrates an outstanding spirit of service in mentoring, sharing and leading others in the mystery writing community. In 1996, he won the Nancy Pickard Mystery Fiction Award for short fiction.

Read more at www.russhall.com.

About the Publisher

Dear Reader,

We hope you enjoyed this book. Please consider leaving a review on your favorite book site.

Visit https://RedAdeptPublishing.com to see our entire catalogue.

Don't forget to subscribe to our monthly newsletter to be notified of future releases and special sales.

www.ingramcontent.com/pod-product-compliance
Lightning Source LLC
Chambersburg PA
CBHW050523190726
48284CB00003B/917